I0563959

Ana

by

Kate Cumiskey

Finishing Line Press
Georgetown, Kentucky

Ana

ACKNOWLEDGMENTS

I am grateful to Finishing Line Press for patience, professionalism, and tender care for my words. Mike Brewer is unfailingly supportive with his gift of an eclectic, peaceful working space. You have reminded me, Mike, of why Mikel and I so love New Smyrna Beach. Jewel Dickson, Teresa Daly, and Alycia Severson generously donated their time as advance readers of the manuscript. Thank you my friends. Philip Gerard never failed me as teacher, friend, mentor, critic. Philip's words are a treasure. Courtney and Kelly Canova worked seamlessly together to capture my character in their portraits. My husband Mikel's love, care, and candor sustain me from middle-of-the-night first words to finished book and beyond. Our son Mikel's haunting images, including his anonymous Ana on the cover, remind me beauty is everywhere if we just choose to see it. Finally to all of the young men and women who've shared their journeys with us by sharing our home and table, thank you for trusting us. You enrich our lives, and we love each of you. Onward.

Publisher: Leah Huete de Maines
Editor: Christen Kincaid
Cover Art: Mikel Cumiskey, Jr., photographer
Author Photo: The Canovas Photography, Kelly and Courtney Canova
Cover Design: Elizabeth Maines McCleavy

Order online: www.finishinglinepress.com
also available on amazon.com

Author inquiries and mail orders:
Finishing Line Press
P. O. Box 1626
Georgetown, Kentucky 40324
U. S. A.

For Margaret McKenzie Davis,
who soldiered on sixteen years
without my father;
and for Jill Gerard

We're all islands shouting lies to each other across seas of misunderstanding.
—*Rudyard Kipling*

Chapter 1

Usually when Ana got to the hospital for her Friday night shift on the ER desk she was in sneakers and workout pants and took a quick shower before she changed into her Pink Lady smock and slacks. She hoped nobody would notice her black dress and ballet flats, touch of lipstick; but the nurses and Charley, the security guard, knew her on sight. Since none of the other volunteers worked weekends Ana suspected somebody would remark on her attire. Sure enough, even though she had a tearful ten-year-old with an ice pack on his wrist and a pair of anxious parents in the triage room, Judee the R.N. on duty called—as Ana scanned her keycard for the door marked EMPLOYEES ONLY—"Looking good tonight, Ana! Out on the town?"

"Just the annual library appreciation dinner."

"Ana, I swear, you're the busiest person in town. They ought to give you a key to the city. Not too bad in here tonight. Pretty slow for a Friday."

Judee turned back to the little boy, Billy Preston. Ana knew him from church. He was the water boy for the J.V. football team; somebody must have fumbled right into him. Ana let door close behind her and headed for the locker room. She passed local Art Guild paintings and photographs in the wide hallway. Her favorite was John Clinton's panoramic shot of the Confederate oak at Old Fort Park, across from the city marina. A wonder it never sold; she'd been here going on four years and that picture greeted her, day and night, on her way to change in and out of uniform.

The locker room was in the old part of the hospital, along with the morgue and the laundry; its door required an old-fashioned key. Ana kept one on her ring. She fished it out of her one and only black pocket book; a leather hobo bag Frank brought back from Quebec years ago. She usually left the purse rolled in a towel on the top shelf of her locker. Ana almost never dressed up and customarily carried a backpack. Before she rewrapped the bag in the towel, Ana took her sneakers, sweat pants, and t-shirt out. She put the sneakers on the floor of her locker, tossed the clothes in the uniform hamper. Saturdays she washed and ironed all the volunteer smocks anyway, and nobody else was going to be in before she did that. Never hurt to add a few of her own things to a load. The budget committee was glad to spring for the washer, dryer, iron, and ironing board when Ana proposed that she do all the uniforms for the week after her Friday shift.

She sat down on the bed—surplus from when the hospital upgraded—to remove her stockings and flats. The flats fit neatly next to her leather bag; the stockings she stashed in the delicates bag hanging from the locker's cross bar. Her own uniform smock and slacks hung on a wire hanger and she took them with her into the bathroom to change, even though nobody else was coming in. She preferred to change in private, not take a chance of an embarrassing moment. Above all things, Ana valued privacy.

Ana liked working the weekend third shift and the staff appreciated it because most volunteers worked days or early evenings, so the paid staff had to screen incomers to the ER themselves at night. Billy had been taken back to the Emergency Room by the time Ana sat down behind the reception desk, and the security guard sat alone in the waiting room watching Fox News. Ana would probably work until about two in the morning unless things got very busy. Generally on the weekends there were a few walk-ins. The more serious cases normally came in by ambulance, bypassing Ana completely.

There were forms to sort from the morning shift. Peggy Phillips and Roger Ahern had worked together; they always left paperwork on the reception desk. Ana gathered the intake forms, scanned her security card for the double doors to the hallway, and slipped them into the inbox for the insurance department to handle Monday morning. She returned to the waiting room to find a bleeding man in the chair, patiently waiting, next to her desk.

"Hello, I'm Ana. I'm sorry I wasn't here when you came in. What's your name?"

"Andy McNamara," replied the man. He had a dirty white t-shirt pressed to his forehead above his right eye, visible scrapes on both elbows. He looked about sixty: he was deeply tanned, with a white beard and mustache and the yellowed eyes of an alcoholic.

"Well, Mr. McNamara, if you don't mind I will just fill out your intake form for you, since your hands are full. You can sign once we get you cleaned up, how's that?"

Something snapped to attention, a sort of puzzlement crossed his face, when Ana said *Mr.* He straightened his spine and pushed back into the chair. "Alright," he said softly.

"Okay, so why don't we start with what happened."

"Well, I fell off of my bicycle. I saw the sign for the hospital, I was right down on Dixie Freeway, and walked my bike here to see if I could get fixed up."

"We'll get a nurse to take a look at you soon." Out of the corner of her eye Ana saw Judee studiously ignoring them. She was great with the locals and tourists with insurance but not so good with drunks and the homeless. Ana, on the other hand, had a talent with the downtrodden patients. "What is your age?"

"Forty-seven."

"Address?"

"Well, ma'am, I'm traveling. I'm just sort of…passing through. I'm originally from Teaneck, New Jersey."

"We get a lot of visitors here from New York and New Jersey. Particularly this time of year and also in winter, when they like to get away from the cold weather. And do you have any insurance?"

"Well," his gaze dropped, "I haven't gotten round to applying down here."

The security guard gave a loud snort, not taking his eyes from the television, beer belly bouncing beneath crossed forearms.

"Okay. Don't worry about that right now. It can be taken care of after you're seen. Here's a worksheet on that; I'll put it with your paperwork. You can complete it at the local library because some of it needs to be done online. It just needs to be done within thirty days of being treated at the hospital. The library is right down the road, about a quarter mile south. Here. You can sign after you get cleaned up; give the hospital copies to the staff back in the ER after that, please, and let me put this bracelet on. Which hand do you write with? Thank you. You can stay right there until the nurse can see you. As you can see, we aren't that busy at the moment."

Ana could see Judee stalling in the triage room and was willing to bet she wasn't charting anything, but playing solitaire on the computer. She smiled at the patient, got up and carried his paperwork to the triage room. Yep, solitaire. Judee closed it with a deep sigh and shot Ana a conspiratorial, put-upon glance: *Don't you just hate dealing with these people?* Ana kept her face carefully neutral. Judee was the professional, after all. Ana was just a volunteer.

"Andy?" Judee called from across the room, not bothering to get up, "In here, please. Let's get your vital signs."

At that moment, the doors to the outside slid open and a pack of teens came in escorting a boy wearing dripping baggies and a rash guard. Night surfing, no doubt. Ana put on a careful smile and handed one of the kids a clipboard with a blank intake form. It might be an interesting night, after all.

Chapter 2

When she was young Ana had been absolutely certain of getting some things right. In the beginning. For instance, when their son was born and Frank was sent to the field by his commander when the baby was three weeks old. She was alone in the house on base at Fort Ord, three thousand miles from everybody she knew; just Ana and the baby. It was easy to get it right. Get it perfect. She knew, absolutely knew that if she got up when he cried and fed and held the baby, if she cleaned his clothes and diapers and skin, held him close, fed him, she was doing it right. Other young mothers on base—Ana was nineteen—argued about on-demand vs. schedule feeding; bottles vs. breast; vaccines. Ana knew with a certainty she'd never experienced before that her instincts were dead-on. It was simple. Whatever the baby needed she supplied. If something she ate upset his tummy she didn't eat it again. Her learning curve was swift; it didn't take books or other mothers or doctors to teach her to stay away from spicy foods, she had it by instinct. She talked to the baby as she'd never spoken to anyone before—confident, quiet, centered, assured.

Her husband laughed, in the beginning, at how her milk squirted across the room at Robin's first tentative cries on waking. Ana immediately mastered her milk supply and while the baby was napping stood in the shower and let her breasts drain in the soothing thrum of hot water.

They were a unit, Robin and Ana. An organism unto itself. Almost from birth, he was like her—sunny, outward-focused. It wasn't until later, when Frank taught him to swim and to surf, that he began to resemble his father. By that time, Ella was small, and things were more complicated. Mistakes had been made.

For some reason, now felt a little bit like that beginning time. Ana was contained, complete on her own. Robin and his wife and sons lived in Washington State, Ella and Thomas and their daughters in Asheville. They seemed to take it in stride that Ana moved to Florida after Frank died; she'd been raised in Flagler Beach, so the beach house south of Robinson always seemed more hers than Frank's to them anyhow. She spent the summers there with the children when they were small, and Frank only joined them for a week, and they always had a Florida Christmas together. Frank loved the waves in winter, the unpredictability of the season. Ana was an excellent swimmer herself.

Since Ana moved full-time to Florida, Robin and Ella and their families came down every July for the week of the fourth. The two couples provisioned the house for a crowd. The last two years, since they were all teenagers, Ana's grandchildren were allowed to spend two weeks in Florida after their parents flew back home. Ana found it easier to be around her grandchildren as teenagers than she had their parents. Of course, everyone was on vacation. But sometimes it crossed her mind that maybe her children were just better parents than she and Frank had been.

When the grandchildren piled into the airport shuttle, brown and windblown and tired, and Ana accompanied them to the airport in Orlando, there were always a few tears. Though she loved them all, Ana was happy to see them off and return to the house to clean and rest and watch the sea. For that month, and two weeks at Thanksgiving and a week at Christmas when she flew to Washington and to Asheville, Ana gave up volunteer work. The pattern appealed to her. The breaks were perfect. She was renewed by her week alone every July with no obligations and enough leftovers to feed herself without having to leave the house.

Nobody ever questioned Ana about how she managed to end up with the beach house after selling the house in Newark to pay for Frank's nursing home and hospital bills. She'd kept a bank account in Florida for almost thirty years. Ana was never one to discuss private matters with her children. She felt a parent's role was to listen, not add to her children's worries with her own. She certainly was young and healthy enough to take care of herself and manage her own affairs, thank Heaven for that. She was even taking classes at the university, free for senior citizens, toward a bachelor's in social work. That was a secret her children didn't know. Being a student gave her a free bus pass, twenty-four hour access to the library and all-night study rooms, and use of the gym and pool. Ana was something of a night owl.

Being a widow was sometimes hard work, but there were perks. People stayed out of your business for the most part—they didn't want to get too close. So, that was good, but lonely, too. Even Ana's own children seemed relieved to have a set pattern of visitation and communication.

They were at a loss as to how to interact with her absent their father. Frank's family had not been in the picture for years, his choice; Ana encouraged him, perhaps too strongly, to stay in touch with his parents and brother and sister. He'd done so sporadically and distantly. Reluctantly, and for her. He made that clear: it was a concession to Ana. She wouldn't know her nieces and nephews on Frank's side of the family if they passed her on the street. Her children had never met their own cousins, and continued to respect their father's wishes as to zero relationships even after his death. It made Ana's life simpler.

The loneliness, missing Frank, Ana was slowly coming to terms with. It would've been impossible to stay in Jersey without him. In Florida she was more in home territory. Although her own brothers and sisters lived out of state and her parents were long dead, Florida was the climate and culture she'd grown up in. It was a strange state; a weird mix of natives and transplants, mostly from New York; and people like Ana who'd been born there, moved away, returned. Having grown up right on the coast she was an avid swimmer. She understood how to deal with the bugs and snakes and sharks and broiling sun. Her father, a rocket designer and Mississippi Depression orphan, taught Ana and her siblings to swim almost before they could walk, spending long summer evenings at the beach with them after driving the hour and a half home from work. He'd looked all over for a house when they moved from Alabama when Ana was four. Hating the smell of the Banana River in Titusville he drove past the bustle of Daytona on the coast road, A1A, until he happened on Flagler. He'd rented a four bedroom concrete block house that same day, and moved the family as soon as school was out, 1961.

Ana enjoyed hot weather more than cold; but when she was a child there were quite a few cold winters in Florida. She loved autumn best, especially October. The beaches were mostly empty then. Just like Flagler in fall used to in childhood, the town of Robinson emptied out and belonged to the locals. The Ovilles, as locals called Orlando weekenders, stayed home and snowbirds hadn't yet left the north. Sometimes she'd teased Frank about being a snowbird, said they had, "two half-Yankee children." Once, on a visit to her father's hometown of Grenada, Mississippi, a lady serving them at a barbecue joint called Mo' Suga' asked Ana, "Honey, where'd you find this Yankee?" when Frank opened his sandwich and wondered aloud at the coleslaw topping the pork.

When they married Frank and Ana seemed to be talking two different languages most of the time. Especially when they argued, which was often. He had a nasal midwestern twang and her Alabama vowels broadened with her temper. His family was northern, Catholic, blue-collar; hers southern, Baptist, white-collar. Hers welcomed him with open arms and big meals where everybody talked and laughed at the same time. His stared at her close-mouthed, frowning, dumb. Once, at lunch at Frank's parents' house when they were dating, Ana tried to fill his father's glass with iced tea. His sister, brother, and mother all jumped and shouted "No!" at the same time. The glass she'd thought full of tea was bourbon, and Ana got a fast education in alcoholism. The house—spotless, cold—was numb as its inhabitants. Frank couldn't leave quickly enough.

Since Frank's death it seemed Ana turned into an entirely other person from her previous self. She was only 58, and had been through the hell of losing him and just about everything else. Ana emerged from grief scalded by it. Before Frank was sick she'd been friendly and scattered and messy; a decent mother, a happy wife, a fantastic cook and good enough housekeeper. She had lots of energy, but it was scattered; when the children were still in school she was always biting off more than she could chew—staying up until one a.m. baking fundraiser cupcakes then getting up at what Frank called the ass-crack of dawn to drive the carpool. Ana had trouble saying no to anybody. After he died, she had trouble saying anything at all.

Everything reminded her of Frank. They'd been together so long, been through so much, that she didn't even attempt to recall who she'd been or wanted to be before him. She simply morphed into a new Ana. One morning she woke up, went to a beauty shop (something she'd never done in her life. Ana had never been pretty, never after junior year of high school agonized over or even thought about it) and had her hair cut off. Frank loved her long hair, hated even when she trimmed off the split ends. One of the last things he'd been able to do was lift a hand and run it slowly through her hair. Ana marched into a shop claiming Walk-ins Welcome! on the door and had her hair cut so short she could wash it with a bar of Ivory soap.

She'd always been plump, a good twenty pounds overweight even on her best days, but after Frank died Ana not only forgot to cook she forgot how to. She forgot to eat. Frank loved her cooking. Some of their finest moments happened around preparing or eating meals—breakfast in the nook at the old-fashioned aluminum table with the yellow vinyl top, patterned with boomerang shapes; lunches where she garnished bright Fiestaware plates with radish rosettes or slivers of crudités. Long, candlelit dinners at her grandmother's cherry table, their faces and the candlelight reflected like a promise in the glass of the matching china cabinet.

Her daughter noticed Ana not eating the week after the funeral, then, on a visit a month later, grew alarmed when she saw her mother. Ana had lost the extra twenty and then some. It seemed eating was physically impossible and she was barely subsisting on three things; cheerios, skim milk, and roasted sunflower kernels, all which Frank couldn't tolerate even the smell of. Then, at the bank one day, Ella noticed her mother go over to the little table where the manager was handing out free Friday hotdogs and coffee in Styrofoam cups. Ana took one of each, a paper napkin and a packet of mustard, and ate lunch absentmindedly while Ella put a couple of hundred dollars, just to help out, in her mother's checking account.

Back in the car, Ella asked, "Mom, you know I'm a little worried about you not eating. There's practically nothing in the house, and I have never seen you eat a hot dog in my life. I thought you hated mustard? We never had it at home? I mean, I'm glad you ate that one, since you didn't have any breakfast this morning, but you've really lost just too much weight. And your hair! It's gone. Your clothes. What's going on?"

Ana looked out the window. "It was your dad who hated mustard. I could always take it or leave it, and since even the smell bothered him— you know how he was about smells, he'd turn right around and leave a restaurant which even served oatmeal—I just never had it around." She stopped for a minute, looked over at Ella driving, looked down shyly then looked away; an unfamiliar, timid, *self-contained* slant to her head, "I keep meaning to make myself eat, but even just being in the kitchen without him causes me such pain the thought of eating is too much. I'm overcome with this, *tiredness,* at the thought. I've tried eating in the living room, on the porch; nothing works. I've even made myself go out. But we loved eating out together, too! It's not like I couldn't do it, before—eat out alone. We had those years apart, that bad patch before we got remarried, had you. Two years. I ate out alone! But now, Ella, I can't. I can't go to church. I can't go to the supermarket." Ana looked down at her hands, folded in her lap on top of her black sweatsuit pants. "I'm not going to talk about the hair. As far as the clothes, nothing fits. I'm giving away most of my old stuff with your dad's things. I have a few easy dresses and I love these sweat suits. If I want to dress up a little more I can put on jeans and a t-shirt. I'm comfortable. And I don't care how I look."

Ella called her brother that night. He had to trade off with her the next week, come pick up the things he wanted out of the house. Robin said,

"You know, with the hotdog and the mustard and all, it sounds like maybe she can eat things Dad couldn't. Like, a psychological thing. Maybe, just maybe, if you could take her someplace they never went. Somewhere not a diner, or a restaurant. Maybe a fast food joint? I doubt they ever went to McDonald's, for Pete's sake. Or Wendy's. Get her a Frosty! I'll bet she doesn't know what one is."

The next day, after gathering boxes at the liquor store, Ella casually drove through and ordered a Frosty and a cup of chili. She handed Ana the Frosty and a spoon, and Ana ate it as absently and methodically as she had the hot dog at the bank, the day before. That night Ella took her mother across town to a biker bar. They sat at a high-top and ate chicken wings and drank seltzer water. She knew for a fact her parents had never darkened the door of a bar—her father had a childlike terror of alcohol—and Ana not only ate six wings, she ordered a side of fries.

Ana wasn't stupid. She knew Ella was just worried about her. In an insulated, remote way she was concerned herself. She knew she was supposed to keep going. Those were the rules. You kept going. She'd never been a self-indulgent, self-focused person. Everybody lost, at least everybody who risked enough to love. It was a matter of time. And by the time Robin came the following week she'd translated the discovery of being able to eat things, and at places, that she and Frank never had together into other ways of remaining. Of doing. Although she wanted nothing more than to lie around the house, sleep as much as she could, she knew that couldn't last. She gradually became purposeful, organized. She made a list every day and allowed herself the small reward of crossing off each task as it was accomplished. After Robin went home Ana joined a gym and developed a routine there. She took headphones and tucked them in the pocket of her workout sweats, attached to nothing—she wanted nobody to speak to her or get too friendly—and walked 45 minutes on the treadmill. She then swam five laps in the pool, showered, washing her hair with the body wash from the dispenser in the locker room. Ana found she liked not only her new, slimmer figure—mainly because it was a body Frank had never seen and even the familiar shape in the mirror of her own breasts had been enough to take her legs out from under her with grief—but especially the exhaustion after a hard workout, which caused her to sleep like the dead; dreamless, hard.

The months wore steadily by. Ana hoed out the house and hollowed herself. Her old friends gradually dropped away, the few who'd been able to stand the horror and sadness of Frank's illness and Ana's focused care. She'd had no time for anyone else for over two years so few people remarked on her transformation. She became someone else.

Only with her grandchildren was Ana a glimmer of her old self. They met her in Florida for the annual vacation, and she travelled to their homes for Thanksgivings, Christmases. Children, Ana knew, were wizards of change, masters of it. They accepted the mysteries of adults' physical and practical changes as unquestioningly as they expected their hearts and habits to stay the same. This she found easy to meet. Ana had always spent separate time with the grandchildren in summer. Frank came down late in June for a week and in August for the last long weekend before they returned north together. Now, at the winter holidays in the midst of her children's families' traditions, it was easier to engage without heartsickness. The happiness and festivities of the holidays were routines like strings of light linking her to others. The rest of the time, the contained Ana moved through days more and more solitary. She mastered widowhood like she used to learn a new recipe.

Because like most people Ana's children were busy, it wasn't all that difficult for her to achieve the level of privacy she needed. She wanted to be alone. Because she set routines for her time spent with them—July in Florida, as usual, even before she sold the house in Jersey and Ana moved there—and Christmas with one and Thanksgiving with the other, the rest of her time became her own. Once she moved to Florida a year after burying Frank everyone else she'd known fell away. She kept a loose correspondence with one old friend, Catherine.

Moving to Florida, volunteering at the hospital and library and a church there, Ana continued her inexorable path to near invisibility. It was what she wanted. She liked quiet; she enjoyed her new fitness and her slow progress at the university. The classes were free. She took them two at the time. One of the first things she'd done in Florida was get her GED. Frank had been the only person alive besides Ana's own siblings who knew she'd left high school to marry and to put him through school. Because widowhood was a natural insulator secrets were easier than ever to keep. Loneliness was new but at least it was her own. She didn't have to project it on anyone and she still wasn't ready for new friends. Working as a Pink Lady at the hospital was like donning a mask; people looked at you and saw what they wanted to see. Depending on the person, a volunteer was a reflection of themselves and their attitudes. A secure person saw a resource within a frame limited by role. The insecure saw someone less than themselves. Ana was surprised that more of the doctors than the nurses tended to sneer and look down. The techs and orderlies, in her opinion, were some of the most competent and professional people in the hospital. But what did she know?

Ana worked until things slowed on Friday and Saturday nights. On Saturday mornings from about 11 until two she washed, dried, and ironed uniform smocks for the rest of the volunteers. Since she liked news she kept the TV in the locker room tuned to a cable news channel, usually CNN, while she ironed. Every shift she worked Ana got a voucher for a free meal in either of the hospital cafeterias, so before doing the laundry she usually ate a late breakfast. Coffee, tea, and soup packets were always free of charge for the public as well as staff, so she often took a cup of tea back to the locker room. There were usually baked goods someone had brought in during the week on the table there, to snack on. Since moving to Florida Ana's appetite had changed drastically. Although she tended to prefer healthy things rather than the carbs she used to favor and cook, institutional food had an almost masochistic appeal. It was as if even her taste buds changed. She never cooked and doubted she would remember how if she tried. That part of her, like her marriage, was gone.

Chapter 3

On Mondays Ana cleaned the beach house. She thought of it as *the beach house* even now with the house in Jersey long gone. Because Ana was raised in Florida, because she was comfortable with the flora and fauna and knew how to navigate, Frank and the children always acted like the beach house was hers. This was one of the reasons she supposed Robin and Ella put up no argument when she asked for their help cleaning out and selling the house up north. It amused Ana how they assumed she and Frank were genteelly affluent because of this house. When they were in elementary school and things were particularly tight, before Frank began his career, they kept saying *just sell the beach house*. It was the same thing they brought up when Frank first came out of the hospital but was too sick to come home and needed skilled nursing care. Ana knew from the beginning of Frank's illness that she'd have to do something to cover what insurance wouldn't and nobody argued with selling the Jersey house. Without Frank Ana didn't fit there. The rooms echoed his absence.

After spending Friday and Saturday working at the hospital and Sunday evening at church serving supper then cleaning up, Mondays were Ana's time alone. She found it difficult to be idle so cleaning the house, even if there wasn't much to be done, was her down time. The trash and recycle had to be out to be picked up by ten a.m. If she had to be somewhere early Monday she put them out Sunday night. Otherwise, at nine she wheeled the can to the curb and set out the green recycle bin. The driveway faced the ocean. A narrow street in front ran along a line of low dunes which were supposed to offer some protection from storms. Most houses had a private walkway to the Atlantic shore over the dunes. At the end of every intersecting street was a public-access crossover. Ana used the time taking the bin down to check the curbs of other houses as far up and down the arrow-straight street as she could see. About 75% of the homes were vacation rentals. A local realty had the market for that cornered, here, and

JACKSON REALTY signs dotted the street. They had numbers underneath: to her south were Jackson's #75 and #33; to the north, #2, then a privately owned vacation home, then #14 and #27. If there were no cans or bins in front the rental had been vacant the previous week. A cleaning franchise called Daisy Clean had all the Jackson houses. Ana saw a Daisy Clean van in front of #75. There were cans in front of #27 and #14 which meant they'd both been rented the previous week or perhaps just the weekend. August was what passed for the slow season for tourism in this part of Florida. Over in Orlando there was no slow season anymore. The theme parks had recently converted to trying to keep visitors cool with cold water misting devices, outdoor fans, and leaving strategically-placed store doors opened wide to pump out air-conditioning. The beaches were quickly catching up to the interior for zero visitor down-time. Still, today on Atlantic Avenue looked quiet. Ana didn't see another soul when she put the trash out.

Next, Ana put towels in the washer. She always washed them before the sheets since they took longer to dry. The living room was upstairs, with a double set of French doors opening onto the deck facing the sea. Ana didn't mind cleaning the panes of the doors. The salt smudged them up almost daily. She used her own concoction of vinegar and water with a couple of drops of lemon concentrate. Today she only needed to clean the outside of the panes. The insides were spotless. That would wait until the sun was directly overhead so she could do it in the shade cast by the eaves. While she wiped down the stove and refrigerator Ana listened to the news and watched the ocean, which she could see easily across the living room. She'd learned to read the sea from her father and could tell today would remain cloudless and warm. She might take a swim before her sociology seminar tonight if she got the house done. She caught the bus into town at 4:30.

Ana liked the news on while she worked. This morning there was a story on about how different states worked to solve homelessness. New York a few years back apparently rounded up homeless individuals, put them on airliners, and flew them to Hawaii. Hawaii eventually flew them back. Ana wondered idly if the people on the planes had to pay for meals or only got free sodas, coffee, water, and snacks. That was a really long trip. Utah on the other hand recently enacted a more successful solution. The state built tiny-house villages for the homeless, saving millions of dollars in now-obsolete crisis intervention and care services. Ana wondered if she could work this story into her paper, then decided against it; the final draft was already turned in and she didn't have a computer at the house to use to revise it anyway.

The living room was on the second floor along with the kitchen, a bathroom, and both bedrooms. Below was a double garage with the washer and dryer, a half bath, and a small room with bunk beds. The stairwell was on the outside of the house, on the north, and when there were teenagers in the house they liked to stay in the bunk-room and pretend they were in their own apartment. Ana left the bunk beds unmade with a plastic cover on each mattress to keep it from getting musty unless she knew they were going to be used. Now, when she went down to the garage to throw the towels in the dryer and sheets in the washer, she went into the bunk-room and flipped on its small air conditioner to air things out a bit. The only window in the room faced west. In the mornings, even without the air on, this room was surprisingly cool. She supposed it was the combination of tile floor and concrete block walls. If any bedroom would flood in a storm this would be it. The house was on a small rise and the short back yard sloped down to a snarl of palmetto, scrub oak, and Spanish bayonets which screened out traffic passing on A.1.A. Ana slid the blinds open and left the bedroom door cracked, which would remind her to close them and turn the air off when she came down to get the last load out of the dryer before school.

After cleaning the bathroom upstairs Ana did the window sills in the bedrooms, bath, and kitchen and the panes on the deck. She set a can of Campbell's potato soup to simmering while she worked and as she ate went over the paper she'd written for class. The teacher already had a copy but Ana kept one anyway. She was proud of the work she was doing. Tonight's was the final class for summer and the students had been assigned an informal data-gathering on a social problem of their choosing. Ana picked homelessness. As she read she thought of Mr. McNamara. Her paper was finished before he'd visited the hospital on Friday night. She'd simply gathered data on the homeless, the insured, and the uninsured as best she could—numbers only, she didn't want to break any privacy laws—and done a bit of research on Monday nights in the twenty-four hour library at the U. As Ana read her paper she felt irrationally sad she hadn't counted Mr. McNamara under the homeless individuals represented in it; as if being numbered might help him somehow. She laughed to herself, put her paper in her backpack, cleaned her dishes and went down to throw the linens in the dryer. She had time for a nap or a swim before catching the bus. Ana chose a nap and set her watch alarm for four o'clock before snapping off the TV and lying down on the couch. By now the sun was overhead and not streaming through the French doors. It was dark and cool in the living room with the blinds drawn.

When Ana woke she brushed her teeth, made a cup of tea, went downstairs and into the garage and got the master bedroom linens from the dryer then went back upstairs and put them on the bed. She drank her tea while she set the thermostat to 80 degrees upstairs, gathered her backpack, keys and phone, and checked the house to make sure all the windows were locked and everything was neat. She washed her cup and put it away, went back downstairs to shut off the bunk-room air conditioner and put up the trash can and recycle bin; washed her hands in the downstairs bathroom, and walked down the street to Flounder Avenue, the cross street to A.1.A, to catch the 4:30 bus.

There was a small shelter with a bench inside it at the bus stop. The three sides were clear Lucite, or supposed to be, but seasons of blowing sand scoured the plastic opaque. Nobody else was waiting. Ana sat in the small shade of the shelter. The sides were supposed to be protection against rain, and the roof, from sun; the shelter was ingeniously designed to accept the breeze off the sea by being open on the east. There were also wide openings around the posts which helped draw what wind there was through and vents at the roof for rising heat. Elevated on a concrete slab, The little room had a terrific view of the end of the island to the south. Ana could see the graceful taper of lush plant life three miles away where the river met the sea. It was easy to spot the bus when it was coming. The shelter was eight feet off the ground atop a public restroom which had an extended concrete pad next to it for bus patrons who couldn't climb stairs and a bench sheltered by the eaves. Ana always waited up top unless there was lightning. A good design for a hot climate. Her father, an engineer, would have liked that.

Ana liked riding the bus. This was one of the few things which reminded her of her life up north—taking public transportation. Haven Beach was ten miles south of town, the university five miles south of the bridge on the mainland. The bus ride was long even though from the shelter Ana could see the university across the mangrove swamp and the Intracoastal. Haven was the southernmost finger of the end of the island, with just a few fish camps before the National Seashore. It was very narrow where the beach house was: the dunes, narrow road, house, then A.1.A,—just two lanes—then a few houses to the river. At the south end of the Seashore river met sea. The bus went to the park gate before turning around in the visitor's center parking lot then heading back north. There were three stops on the island after Ana's: at the shopping center; at the one intersection with a Walgreens and a liquor store and a surf shop and a hardware store, then in front of Mangroves, the fanciest restaurant on the beachside, before the bridge spanning the Indian River. Then, a few stops heading down U. S. 1 before the bus turned inland and headed the mile up Tenth Street to the main entrance to East Florida University.

Ana had half an hour before class started. It was only 5:30. She went to the library to check her e-mail. All she had was a note from Robin giving her the information on her ticket voucher for her trip in November to Bellingham and one from her sociology professor. Robin always scheduled her trip early because he worked for the railroad and the trains were fairly busy at the holidays. She got a free trip to Bellingham and back complete with meals and sleeper. This year she'd agreed to stay two weeks. Robin and Marie were taking a trip of their own after Thanksgiving. Ana would stay with the children and their two golden retrievers, Maud and Matilda. She'd leave DeLand on November 14th in the afternoon, arrive back on the 8th of December in the morning. Perfect for the bus schedule to and from Haven Beach. The train station was inland twenty miles, just west of the county seat on the St. John's river, but the bus system ran county-wide.

Ana found train travel both exciting and restful. She enjoyed the luxury of being served her meals where she chose, in her compartment or in the dining car, and the courtly manner she was treated with as family of one of the crew. Robin got two free trips a year as a railroad worker and made the most of them, using one as a gift to his mother. Before Frank died Ana used to go out for a week just before school started to stay with Robin's family, a much shorter trip from New Jersey. Ana and Frank never had time for train travel together. It was something she was used to doing alone.

The note from Dr. Brewster requested Ana stop by his office before class or, if she had time, after. Ana signed off the computer and headed to Brewster's office. His door was open, he looked pleased when she tapped on it.

"Ana! Come in. This will only take a moment." Professor Brewster was about her age, in his late fifties; tall and thin with a neat gray mustache and beard and what looked to have once been a mess of dark curls, now mostly gray.

" I wanted to discuss something with you outside of class because it doesn't really have to do with this class. I'm sure you'll know you are getting an A on your final paper since we worked on that draft together and you had few changes to make. Your topic interested me very much. I would like for you to consider taking my graduate seminar in local sociological issues next semester. I know you're a junior taking two classes at a time; I've looked at your transcript. Your informal study of local homeless rates through volunteer work at the hospital is something which deserves deeper consideration. I'm sure you know about the hot argument going on in the Robinson city government about this very issue—the factions developing. There are those who want to not only shut down the local churches' food banks but make both hitchhiking through on U.S. 1 and even accessing the two edible public parks illegal for those who don't have local identification. I'd like your ideas to be a part of this seminar, which is spearheading studies for the city council."

Ana wasn't sure how she looked but she was struck dumb. It was just a paper! Oh how she hated attention, being singled out! If she could she'd blend in with the wall. Dr. Brewster must've mistaken her silence for consideration.

"If you are worried about credit, you can either choose to use this as an elective credit or bank it for grad school. I do hope you will consider grad school; you're a shoo-in. Ana, if people like us don't work on these concerns this marginalized population will just become more so. They have fewer and fewer opportunities to speak for themselves, and it is up to those of us with advantages to do the elbow-work of educating our fellow citizens. Florida, rightly, has a huge homeless population; people come here so they don't freeze to death! You've hit on some interesting ideas with your discussion of how differently these people are treated in the emergency room. If the local council has its way they won't even be allowed to move through town, much less access services here. I think you and other concerned Haven Beach residents should be a part of the discussion."

"Haven Beach?" Ana finally spoke. She felt stupid. It was all she could think of to say.

"Oh, I thought you knew, we're practically neighbors. I see you at the bus stop at the end of Flounder on my way in on Mondays. I've thought of offering you a lift but I didn't want to seem forward."

" I like the bus. I didn't realize you lived down there."

"Yes, at the beach end of Grouper. Well, I hope you'll consider it. We should get to class." Dr. Brewster turned to pick up his briefcase from the floor near the bookcase.

"Dr. Brewster, I just can't. I take fall off to travel every year. In fact I just got my schedule for my November trip in my e-mail, at the same time

I received your note. I couldn't cancel now. My family is looking forward to this and so am I. It's all set. But I appreciate your thinking of me."

"That's disappointing. I do this same seminar every fall, maybe next year? We really need your ideas now, early in the semester, before the council elections in January. Could you consider coming to speak to the other students, say, in early October?"

Ana stood up, both hands nervously clutching her pack by the handle at the top. "I'll think it over. Can you send me a little more information about the seminar, maybe the syllabus, and about what the council is doing, over e-mail? I'm doing a lot of traveling. I'm not sure I'll have the time." She had absolutely no intention of speaking to a class of grad students or a bunch of local politicians, but neither did she have any idea how to gracefully get out of this situation. Thank God she already had her train schedule so she didn't have to tell a white lie, or worse, the truth.

Chapter 4

Ana got to the auditorium later than usual. She'd learned through painful trial and error where to sit but her preferred spot fifth row from the front on the aisle was taken. She went back a few rows and was able to get an aisle seat. The auditorium seats were comfortable and it was usually cold; she kept an old-fashioned shawl in her pack. She'd learned when she first started college not to sit in the back. Students there slept (and snored), clacked away on computers and tablets and phones, even watched TV. Closer to the front they tended to pay better attention, with students who were actively engaged sitting right on the front row.

"Well, I can see a lot of students saved up one of their absences for the last class," Professor Brewster started out, "which is a bit of a shame as we have some interesting things to discuss. As you know the final is next Monday evening. For those of you who chose to attend tonight, I have a bonus question for the final which will give you an additional ten points if thoroughly answered. But, you need to stay until the end of this lecture and pay attention to know what to do for that."

Ana looked around the dim auditorium. There were one hundred and four students in the class. It seemed about half of them were present. There were two empty seats next to Ana, then a boy of about twenty who had been texting on his phone until Dr. Brewster said *bonus*. The boy punched the shoulder of another sitting directly in front of him, who'd been slumped down as if he were sleeping. "Bonus points!" whispered the first boy to the other. He put his phone in his shirt pocket and sat up straighter. So did his friend.

"As you know," continued the professor, "your final papers are due tonight. Several of you took advantage of having me go over your rough drafts to offer suggestions and corrections. There are three papers in particular which I was impressed with and these are the topic of my lecture. I won't embarrass the students who came up with these ideas by telling you who they are. But I will tell you all three have been invited to participate in my fall graduate seminar. That's unusual, but this was an unusually excellent class. For the most part. The sociology department is heavily involved in local issues; that's the focus of the fall grad seminar. In fact it was one of my undergrad students from this very class—just a few years ago—who came up with using the old high school property on the causeway as well as the old water treatment plant site as edible parks. Think about that next time you are eating a free navel orange on your way over to the beach or picking a couple of avocados for your next batch of guacamole. That project started as a term paper and continued as the focus of the student's thesis in graduate school.

"Now I want to tell you about these most recent papers. One student studied the green bike program after visiting his brother out in Waldport, Oregon. He decided to see if he could replicate it here. He went to the bike shop over at the beach on Third Avenue. They agreed to fix up a couple of old bikes and supply helmets. You may have noticed the green bikes with baskets on the front. There's a laminated sheet at the bottom of the basket which describes what is expected of users. It's pretty simple. You use the bike as needed, then leave it tied to a bike rack with the yellow nylon cord provided if you are going to use it again. When you're done with the bike, you leave the helmet in the basket and wrap the cord around the seat post instead of tying it up. This lets the next user know the bicycle is up for grabs. If you're going to use one of the bikes it is recommended you wear a hat under the helmet. There are two of the bikes around town. Any user can take one to the bike shop at any time service is needed. One might suppose that they'd be stolen or vandalized. So far these two have been on the streets of Robinson for fourteen weeks and it seems they are being used appropriately. Each has been brought in for service a couple of times already, and not by the student who designed the program. Wonderful.

"Another paper dealt with one of our big local issues; overcrowding. As anyone who has tried to get to or from the island in a hurry on a weekend knows, all the advertising by the advertising authority has resulted in tourists descending not only from the Orlando area but from all over the world. While once our town was quiet at least part of the year, you know as well as I do that time is over. It's wall-to-wall people seven days a week, twelve months of the year. A huge conglomerate has successfully persuaded the planning and zoning board—which now consists entirely of people who lived out of state most of their lives, and moved to town basically to get rich and avoid state taxes where they came from—to waive ordinances which limited use of land along the beach, allowing them to put up several new high-rise hotels. The resulting crowds have filled, and caused the addition of, restaurants in town to the point where city parks are now being used to courtesy valet customers' cars. The municipal boat ramp parking lots fill every day with cars valeted there from these restaurants. Local fishermen can't leave their vehicles and trailers there. There's nowhere for them to park.

"The position of the corporations bringing in the people, and the restaurants and hotels, is that all that money coming in brings jobs to the town and is good for the locals. My student did a study of all of the local employees working at the two new hotels and the three under construction as well as the two new five-star restaurants on the beach. He found that not a single employee beyond the project and general managers—all of whom were brought to town from up north—has any benefits whatsoever. No health care, no retirement, no sick days. And all of these new positions, because they are minimum wage or below jobs, have actually brought the per capita income of the town down rather than raising it. Fascinating. This topic too bears further study and certainly needs publication for the eyes of the community. People need to understand that the rhetoric spouted by those developers crowding houses onto lots on the causeway access roads and getting hotels put up on the beach is doing much more harm than good to the town of Robinson.

"The last paper I want to bring up dealt with exploring the attitudes of local professionals at the hospital toward homeless and uninsured patients as opposed to patients with insurance and addresses. Informal data was gathered regarding waiting time for treatment and number of courtesy words, *please, thank you, yes sir, yes ma'am* with these populations; as well as use of first name as opposed to last name with a personal pronoun. The results were sad but not surprising. I have asked the student who wrote this paper to consider doing a guest lecture early in the upcoming semester. As anyone who reads the local paper knows, the issue of how to respond to the needs of the homeless here is the leading issue in the upcoming city elections. If this student agrees to give a talk I'll get an ad into the paper and it will be up on the university website, so keep your eyes open for that. Okay, let's open up for questions and comments."

A girl in the front row raised her hand. "The homeless thing bothers me. I've noticed that some of the homeless people in town try to come into the U library, particularly at night, and the security guard stops them. But this one lady I see all the time up on the fifth floor, the quiet floor, in the women's room. There's a couple of couches in there and this lady crashes and sleeps up there sometimes in the middle of the night. The guards are men so I guess if she can get past them she's pretty safe up there. I don't see the harm in that. That's what the couches are in there for right, for people to rest and be safe?"

The boy a couple of seats from Ana leaned down to his friend and whispered, "That's not what those couches are for. They're put there so our bitches can get rested up." His friend gave an appreciative head bob and chuckle.

A male voice from the back called out, "But that's not fair! There aren't couches in the men's room up there. Why do they get couches and we don't?"

"Well," Dr. Brewster responded, "that might be a question for another forum or one for the dean of students, but for now let's continue the discussion about homeless people on campus. It is interesting that what *appears* to be a homeless individual is able to rest in relative safety in the library women's room. But think about this. Are there homeless individuals on campus who are also students? I'll tell you, there are. There are actually a couple of students I know for a fact are homeless—right here in this class. Naturally I won't be singling them out. But it begs the question, what exactly is homelessness? Does couch surfing qualify? And how many of you would be homeless if your grades came out and your parents pulled their tax information from your FAFSAs? After all, if you live on campus—or even off—doesn't your financial aid, which is tied to most of your parents' tax returns, provide for that?" Ana saw both boys down the row from her look uncomfortably at each other, all seriousness now. "Where would you be without those public dollars? It's something to think about. Especially with your vote."

Ana had trouble listening to the rest of the discussion. She couldn't help thinking that Frank would have gotten a kick out of her predicament. Dr. Brewster had *not* said anything about her giving a public talk when they met in his office! It was pure coincidence Ana's paper studied something which was a hot topic in town; she rarely picked up a newspaper and she certainly didn't keep an eye on local politics. What a pickle. She'd have to send a polite note to Dr. Brewster.

Ana wondered what he'd meant when they met in his office, about not wanting to seem forward when he mentioned being neighbors. Was he interested in her? It was true he always called her "Ana," and with the other students he used "Mr." and "Ms.", but that was something she'd experienced with a lot of other classes in college, something she disliked. Professors who were closer to her age than to the other students' tended to treat her like a peer. It was awful. Sometimes they seemed to expect her to share their knowledge base or offer instruction right along with them in class discussions. In one poetry class, when a young student had written a sexually graphic, supposedly humorous poem about a husband's penis falling off and the wife grieving over the loss of this *most important digit,* the professor, flustered, asked Ana if she wanted to explain to the young poet why this might not necessarily be a believable line!

Because Ana had never been pretty she'd several times made the mistake of getting too comfortable in the company of men. She'd grown up with brothers so she got along with men. She'd always been around them. But from a young age she assumed her ugliness offered a sort of freedom to be close to men and safe from their advances, which hadn't played out to be true. In high school when looks mattered a great deal she'd been safe in the company of her brothers and their friends. She'd always assumed that was because of her looks. Now she knew better. As an adult, more than once she'd misled a friend into thinking she was interested in an affair. This always came as a nasty shock to Ana; that a man she was friends with could want her. *But, I'm not pretty!* She'd say. Frank would laugh at her, shake his head, say, *What you don't understand about men is an awful lot.*

Ana determined to avoid any time alone with Dr. Brewster. She wasn't taking any chances. Her life as she'd built it was carefully constructed and ran pretty well. It depended on privacy and routine. She wasn't about to disrupt either. Determining that, Ana tuned back in to the class.

"Here's your bonus assignment for the final. You need to choose one of the three papers we discussed, summarize it, and give your own ideas about what can be done to rectify either of the last two situations, or help the bike program be a success. See you all next week for the final. Remember, if you have a 92% or better on everything you've turned in so far, and you know you are getting an A on your paper, you can skip the final altogether."

When Ana left class it was after nine o'clock. By habit—even though she was one of those students technically done with the class; she had her A—she walked to the main library. Although the campus was fairly new Ana loved it. The sidewalks were wide and meandering rather than straight, as if to imply a stroll rather than a rush to class. There were benches everywhere. The university was built on hammock land rather than sandhill pine so old live oaks trailed streamers of Spanish moss.

At night the solar ground lights around the roots of the trees made dim and glowing patterns, like stars flung across a sky. Usually on Mondays—she always took classes on Mondays and Thursdays—Ana worked on her assignment for the next week straight through until it was finished, occasionally until morning. Tonight she couldn't keep her mind from the comments made by the students. The girl seemed so sincere, questioning, so serious, wondering why it was okay for some homeless people to take refuge on campus but not others. Ana couldn't see her face, but her posture, the way she threw herself backward in her seat in surprise, made Ana think she hadn't contemplated the notion of homeless students. For the most part—even though this was a public university—the students here behaved as if they were privileged. Ana knew from experience most of them were.

Frank hadn't finished college. Try as they might they could only afford a couple of years of community college early in the marriage. It wouldn't have occurred to either Frank or Ana to depend on their parents for help. They'd married early, against their parents' wishes. Frank joined the army so they could, and they barely scraped by in California. After, they'd come to Florida and he worked construction in Jacksonville. She managed a Laundromat during the evenings, he took classes. He was proud of the work he did in college as Ana was now. It occurred to her not for the first time that those who struggled through college on their own funds seemed more appreciative of the education than those who had it handed to them. That was a sociological question which might interest Dr. Brewster.

When Ana looked around here, she did see some students who appeared to be struggling. A few she'd seen on campus came to the free bread Fridays at church and the Wednesday suppers. There was a Methodist church in town which set up two long tables on weekdays near the student union and gave out plates of cornbread with collard greens. It wasn't the students who ordered lattes and bakery-fresh bagels with flavored cream cheese in the bookstore café who stood around those tables after morning classes. But, most of the students at East Florida were of the latte variety. Ana herself looked more like one of the professors and was sometimes mistaken for one. Her short silver hair was striking; since she'd joined the gym after Frank died she'd kept up her exercise routine. She used the gym at school and loved to walk on the beach and along the causeways over the river and back. She could wear the loose, pajama-style pants and thin t-shirts popular in the warm months here, and comfortable sneakers. Most of the students wore t-shirts and jeans. Ana kept a floaty black sweater in her pack and a shawl; classrooms and auditoriums were invariably cold. Maybe to keep students awake during lectures.

Each semester Ana noticed at least a few men her age or older who were new to the campus. They stuck out. The reason she noticed these men and knew they were new students was mostly their demeanor, which changed by the end of the semester. They had spanking-new backpacks, loaded down, and wide eyes. They overdressed in the hot months and underdressed for the coldest auditoriums. They looked out of place and uncomfortable everywhere from the pathways under the trees to the classrooms to the bookstore and library. Ana knew from her sociology classes that these were "displaced workers." There was even a spot for that on the Federal Application for Student Aid, or FAFSA. Displaced workers. Like Frank had been. Ana wondered if Frank would've gone back to college when his career with the railroad went belly-up during the recession if he hadn't gotten sick. Probably. After all, he had a few semesters of community college credit from when they were kids. What would he have studied? No use wondering on that.

Ana always felt a pang of sympathy when she saw these new (what the admissions office referred to as *nontraditional* or *nontrad*) students. From experience she knew that they either dropped out by the second semester, or (more likely) shed the extra clothes and books and the nervousness and found out a lot about themselves through their college careers. They often arrived with extra pounds and bad habits like smoking, but as they realized their years of hard work and parenting would stand them in good stead through this new venture—as Ana's had— they seemed to grow younger, healthier and more confident. Ana was secretly sure some of the things which bothered her bothered them as well; but they, like she, honed their focus and drove forward, largely ignoring the growing pains and risk-taking, noise and bumbling exploration, of the adolescent population around them.

Most of these older students were men who'd been hit by the economic collapse several years ago, the same one which cost Frank his job. Ana knew this because it was a topic in several of her classes. While students who were new to the U didn't tend to enter discussions about it, more seasoned students readily did. There were some displaced women in the student population too, and some veterans who were older than the right-out-of-high-school crowd. The veterans were a population with their own issues when it came to school; active duty military, too. There was a 24 hour USO lounge as well as a Veteran's Assistance office in the Commons near the bookstore. Some reservists complained in class about having to put off college, which was what they'd enlisted to gain in the first place, for years. They hadn't expected war after war. It made Ana thankful that Frank served in peacetime. Maybe her sociology degree might lead to a job after all. The field was wide-open right now.

Tonight she was at the library almost before she realized it. On a whim Ana took the elevator to the fifth floor. Idly, she wondered if the homeless woman mentioned in class was in the women's restroom. She opened the door. Nope. Both couches—tucked back in a dim, windowless alcove away from the swinging door and the door into the bathroom— were empty. They were old; a warm, chocolaty leather. Ana sat down and sank deep into a couch facing a giant mirror. She was lower, though, than the mirror and reflected she could see the light and dark paths of a copy of Pollock's painting Robin called *the path to God picture* when he was a little boy.

Ana knew, even though she never let herself mull it over, that all of this, everything she had done since Frank's death, was grieving. Maybe someday she'd snap out of it but part of it was that she really didn't care. The beginning of it; cleaning and selling the house, giving the children the things they wanted, even changing herself and coming to Florida, seemed normal. By now she'd moved into a whole other existence. She stuck rigidly to her routine, wanted nothing to do with anybody. All her volunteering and school, all of it was not an effort at connecting or helping or even self-improvement. It was merely a way to continue, a way to push back against Frank's death. Against any death. Her's.

KEEPING THINGS WHOLE

Mark Strand

In a field
I am the absence
of field.
This is
always the case.
Wherever I am

I am what is missing.
When I walk
I part the air
and always
the air moves in
to fill the spaces
where my body's been.
We all have reasons
for moving.
I move
to keep things whole.

For some reason, despite the isolation and subterfuge of Ana's life, in some form she needed to keep things whole. It was why the routine existed:

Friday: Free bread Friday at church, volunteer at the hospital at night

Saturday: do the uniforms, volunteer at night again

Sunday: Church, serve supper and clean-up the kitchen

Monday: Clean the beach house, class

Tuesday: Volunteer at the library, serve at the soup kitchen

Wednesday: Prayer meeting and after service dinner

Thursday: Class

July: host her children and grandchildren for two weeks at the beach house, host grands for one more, week off volunteering to enjoy the beach alone

August: chaperone church teen girls' camp

November: Bellingham trip

December: Asheville trip

It wasn't as if a hurricane or being sick or having to change her schedule threw her off, as long as she managed to keep people away, away. She wondered idly when she'd miss them and wondered too if this was some form of arrogance. She could see people around her engage, try to engage her. She could see them brush up against her brittle shell and away and was fully aware this was what she intended. Sometimes she wondered if she'd snap out of it. If so, what then? Mostly she didn't care.

Chapter 5

When Ana woke up she had no idea what time it was. The restroom alcove was dim. It could be 10 am or 2 am. Her backpack made an unintended pillow, her shawl a perfect blanket. She hadn't even slipped off her sneakers. She must've fallen asleep as soon as she sat down on the leather couch. It was quite comfortable. She had, apparently, wrapped her backpack in her sweater and flipped it to the back, the soft side. It was padded to hold a laptop, very much like a pillow. She'd also wrapped herself in her shawl, but the restroom wasn't kept as cold as the library itself.

Ana stretched, folded her sweater and shawl and unzipped her pack, put them in. She felt disoriented in the perpetual twilight. She took out her toiletries kit and zipped up the pack, slung it over her left shoulder. In the handicapped stall Ana hung up her pack on the hook on the back of the door and put her toiletries kit on the wide sink. After using the toilet, she took her time brushing her teeth and freshening up her hair, washing her face. She considered changing clothes—she kept spare clothes and underthings in her pack—but she wanted to check her e-mail before heading out and figured she could change after that at the gym.

The library was quiet. There was a skeleton crew on but the computer stations, chairs, and stacks were empty of students. It must early morning. Ana chose a computer opposite the eastern wall, where the gray light of dawn was filtering through. A mistake; glare on the screen. She got up and moved down the row to a computer close to the stacks, opposite a wall instead of a window. Ana moved the mouse around and tapped keys randomly until the school website showed up. She wasn't good at understanding computers. It was 6:47a.m.

Dear Dr. Brewster,

Thank you for your kind words about my research paper. I will

keep in mind your invitation to take the graduate seminar next fall, if that is alright. I will discuss with my family perhaps adjusting our travel plans around that next year. For this year, I will be away most of November and most of December. I am not really comfortable with public speaking, so have to pass the honor up of giving a talk. Again, thank you for thinking of me,
Ana Mills

There. Ana felt good about getting the e-mail out of the way. She wasn't sure if it was that or her unexpected night on the library couch but she felt remarkably rested. She might even do an early morning workout at the gym before breakfast. She was hungry. Still, she took a few moments to dash an e-mail off to Robin confirming the dates for her train trip.

Ana daydreamed about her train trip while she did her routine on the treadmill, then swam her laps. Her route this year would take her to D.C. then Chicago, then through the badlands along the Canada border before reaching Seattle. Ana kept her winter things at Robin's and a few with Ella. She wouldn't need much more than her shawl and a warm turtleneck if she stayed on the train, but if she got out to sightsee she'd need warm clothes. The Dakotas were spectacular in winter. She loved to sit in her private room and drink hot tea, cozy with a good book, and doze to the rhythm of the train while watching the winter countryside flash by. One of her favorite things was to watch the faces of people stopped at the railroad crossings as the train went past. She imagined them imagining her, wondering who rode high up on the second floor of the sleeper car. She could see them sometimes, the drivers in their pickups out in the country, in sedans and minivans in the cities, craning to see how long the train was; and children pointing, keeping count of the cars.

When Ana finished her swim she sat for a few minutes in the whirlpool. Then, ten minutes in the sauna followed by a quick shower before catching the bus up to the hospital. By the time she got there most of the breakfast crowd in the employee cafeteria had cleared out. It was only 10:30 so they were still serving breakfast. She ordered a mushroom, Swiss cheese, and onion omelet with sliced tomatoes and hash browns, and drank two cups of coffee with cream and sugar. While she ate Ana read a chapter of the latest book she'd checked out at the library, Donna Tartt's *The Goldfinch*. It was a strange book. Like both of Tartt's previous novels it drew her inexorably in. The characters were richly, incredibly, believably flawed. While the story was a bit fantastical, hard to believe, edgy; the people in it were so deeply human that Ana could almost see them. The details were fine and elaborate—what they wore, what they ate, how the air at a particular time of day on a particular street corner felt on the skin. Wonderful. The chapters were long and complicated and Ana didn't want to quit reading when she was done with her meal, so she took her pack and another cup of coffee and her book to the volunteers' locker room and read for another hour. After all, there wasn't really time to go all the way over to the beach. She was due at the library at 2:00, and it was right down the street. It felt indulgent and wonderful to lose herself in her book in the middle of a Tuesday.

"Ana! How nice to see you. I didn't know you were working today. Are you working today? I should hurry, I'm late. I'm supposed to be up on two in the surgical waiting room from one until five today. I just got to putting a pot roast in the crock pot before I left the house, and it took longer than I thought, I have an new, giant pot and I thought it was a good idea to put in lots of vegetables. Carrots, onions, potatoes. Mushrooms. I'm just going to change real quick. I adore those wonderful track suits or warm up suits or whatever you call them that you wear! They're so svelte! I could never get away with them with my figure. What is that material? Is it rayon or something? So thin and roomy at the same time? Where do you get those? You must have one in every color, but I really like that black. It's kind of elegant and casual at the same time."

Martina Anderson was a pretty, bubbly woman in her forties. She seemed to be a series of various-sized circles. Her black hair curled in half-dollar-sized Os all over her head, framing a round face with a button mouth and large brown eyes. She was right, the suits Ana habitually wore would have looked terrible on her. Martina was curvy everywhere Ana was slim. She disappeared into the restroom and came out in her smock and white uniform pants without ever halting her happy chatter or waiting for an answer to any of the stream of questions.

"Bye now, Ana! I'll see you later, maybe! I finish at five, will you be here?" Ana shook her head, "No? Well, okay. It was wonderful to see you. Enjoy your book." When the door closed behind Martina Ana let out a little chuckle, then a sigh of relief. Martina reminded her of one of those sudden summer showers that happen almost every day during the hot season in Florida; fast and refreshing and leaving as quickly as they came.

Sometimes Ana felt strange about her aloneness. Widowhood offered a cover which allowed an emotional and physical freedom she couldn't have imagined earlier in her life. This was, she supposed, natural;

marriage by definition involved so much which was private between husband and wife. When one of them was gone all that shared experience and emotion became singular and reflective. Gone. Being with a person who'd had all that and lost it was a different thing from spending time with somebody whose habit, whose past, was singular in the first place. People tended to stick strictly in the present with their talk or fill conversation with their own voice as Martina had done. This made it easy to be private, to be quiet, to be present and elsewhere at the same time. Ana found it alarmingly easy to fit into the molds people seemed to hold in their minds, shaped by how they imagined her.

For a long, long time after Frank's death there hadn't been much to Ana. She felt hollowed, devastated, mummified. Still. Her metamorphosis had been deliberate, a survival instinct. She could not have stayed the same person she had been with Frank, without him. She couldn't stay in the same house, the same town. Ella and Robin had not pushed their mother to stay and were fine with her sale of the house. They'd both made several trips to help her sort through belongings, shipping things by train to their own homes, helping her take the leftovers to Goodwill. They each even took some of Ana's winter things, clothes she'd need more in Bellingham and Asheville than in Florida so she had less to pack when she came to visit every winter. Ana'd divided the things she planned on giving to the children someday, and gone ahead and done so after Frank died. After all, she never knew when something might happen to her, as well; then it would be too late.

Her grandmother's furniture had gone to Ella, the bedroom sets from the children's rooms to Robin. They each chose the artwork, dishes, and photographs they wanted. There was very little disagreement. Ana found it funny, the things they treasured. Both wanted the wooden toilet paper holder, the spindle, from the downstairs bathroom and they both wanted the ironing board. All three of them thought it was funny. Neither Robin nor Ella could explain why. Ana let them work it out. Robin took the ironing board, Ella the spindle. It was funny, the things which mattered to people.

Ana moved through the business of closing and selling the Jersey house with a steady precision completely at odds with the scattered, messy person she had always been. Order sustained her. When she got to Florida she treated herself to two weeks, in the off season of August, at the Bella Vista Inn on the western shore of the Intracoastal Waterway. The building was old, single-story concrete block; with ten rooms in a C around a courtyard filled with lush plants, concrete benches, tables with broken pottery faired into the tops, and crooked little gravel paths, and charcoal grills. The owner was grumpy but kept a spotless Inn. The price was low due to being on the river instead of the ocean. Her room, number 8, had a tiny living room with a rattan sofa and chair and TV with cable; a small kitchen, terrazzo floors, icy AC, and a back door with jalousie windows which cranked open to let in the breeze off the river in the late evenings. There was a public park between her back patio and the river. She sat in an Adirondack chair and watched children on the brightly colored plastic slides and swings and see-saws in the evenings.

There were fishing poles and tackle for loan in the motel office, a new T-shaped dock jutting into the Intracoastal beyond the park. Ana walked over the bridge and got a baggie of live shrimp at Red's Bait one evening. Under a full moon she caught two flounder and a red. She let them go but it was good to know she still had the skills of fishing in salt water from her childhood.

The bedroom of her unit had an old-fashioned full-sized bed, but the mattress was the best Ana ever slept on. There was a fully-stocked kitchenette. She bought coffee and eggs and bacon, cheese and bread and butter, hotdogs and canned vegetables. While at the Bella Vista Ana learned how to fix food for just herself. She ate the simple foods of childhood, drank coffee even at night. She slept the deep sleep of recovery, hearing in the night the sounds of the bridge tender signaling boats from the bascule with his low, mournful horn; *wait* or *all clear.*

Every morning Ana crossed the bridge with the morning traffic: the motel maids and restaurant servers and dishwashers, the store clerks and lifeguards and kids who worked in the surf shops passing her in their rusty cars and on bikes and skateboards. This was a town where people of all ages walked, and it had more than its share of geriatrics. The paths along the causeway, over the bridge and to the beach, up Atlantic Avenue and back over the South Bridge, then down Riverside, were wide and well-lit even in the middle of the night. People walked for company; they walked babies and dogs; they walked because their doctors insisted, and they walked to get to and from work. Ana got to know the town while she lived at the Bella Vista in ways she'd never had time to staying at the beach house with the family at Haven Beach, eleven miles south. This was a world apart; the world of the regular townsfolk. The work people. Across the causeway from the Inn were several older, low-slung condominiums from the 1970s, along with several medical arts complexes and some law offices. On the south, the same side as the Inn, there was a bowling alley and a couple of pubs. The condominiums didn't house the changing populace the tall ones along the ocean did but an aging, permanent population of singles and couples in their sixties, seventies, eighties—even a few over ninety. They lived with little dogs and cats and were checked on by visiting nurses, maids, and grown children rushing by on their way home from work. There was a rhythm to the days and nights living on the north causeway which suited Ana. She knew that even after she was settled into the town of Robinson she might occasionally stay at the Bella Vista. Protected by the bulk of the island, it would be a nice hurricane evacuation retreat if she ever had to find one.

After relaxing for a couple of days and getting her bearings Ana went to her bank, First Community, to check up on her funds there. She added a checking account to the small savings account she'd maintained since the children were small. She liked First Community. It was one of those chain banks which tried to be an old-fashioned town bank. They always had daisy cookies which reminded her of Sunday School, and coffee, set out all day long. On Fridays they had hot-dog Friday, free hot-dogs and bags of popcorn. The bank was open 7-7. It also was open until one on Saturdays, and if you kept two hundred dollars in your checking account and one hundred in savings, it had what the staff called Wow Wednesdays.

On Wednesdays, for any purchases made with a debit card from First Community which ended in fifty one cents up to a dollar, the bank put the change up to the next dollar in your savings. If you spent 10.64 on your debit card, they put .36 into savings. If you spent .51, they put .49 in. Ana was thrifty and now alone. She planned carefully and made most of her necessary purchases on Wednesdays. Every penny counted now.

Ana also switched her license. She didn't have a car but she needed to make sure she had local I.D. because she wanted to get established right away with volunteering at the hospital and the library. When school opened she wanted to take advantage of free education for senior citizens at the University. Every day those first two weeks she had some chore, and she took the public bus. The hospital had a series of training videos she had to view, and she had to have drug testing and a background screening for the hospital work. That took a whole day. The library was easier. She got her card, checked out some books, and picked up a volunteer form at the counter. When she returned her books the next week she returned the form. The volunteer coordinator scheduled her to work in the back room checking in books, one day a week, right then and there.

Ana's aloneness accompanied her everywhere. She didn't say much but she had a ready smile and she'd noticed when she was young that people are more comfortable with ugly people than with attractive ones. More at ease. People were easy with her. They seemed to take for granted that she knew what she was about and didn't question her. Nobody asked why she moved to Robinson; where she lived other than for paperwork; why she wanted to volunteer or take classes. She switched from carrying a purse to a backpack. It was easier since she walked so much. She kept a bathing suit and thin towel, a toilet kit and a spare warm-up suit, and clean socks and underthings in her pack along with her wallet rapidly filling with new I.D. cards, her bus pass, her new debit card. She always carried a library book, sunscreen, and a bottle of water. Sunglasses and a hat. And because she never knew when she would need them, her all-purpose, wrinkle-free black dress and ballet flats. She had a cell phone which was part of Robin's family plan. It had a Bellingham area code, but unlimited minutes. Nobody seemed surprised at the odd area code when she was filling out forms; apparently these long-distance family plans were a common thing. Robin got a free fifth line with the four he purchased for himself, Marie, and the kids. Using a cell phone took some getting used to; Ana and Frank kept an old-fashioned hard line. But one of the things Ana liked about it was that hers could be loaded with music, and she had headphones. She liked to walk the paths along the causeway at night listening to jazz, stopping to watch fishermen pull in cats and flounder, sheepshead and redfish from the two small bridges linking the islands of the north causeway.

It took Ana almost no time to get used to being part of a beach town again. She'd grown up in one. One of the first things she did was go to Wal-Mart and buy a sun shelter and a blow-up air mat. Ana liked to spend her free afternoons at the beach. She'd set up the shelter, blow up the mat, open her windows and let the breeze blow through while she read. More often than not Ana fell asleep in the shelter and woke up as dark was falling just in time to pack up her gear, shower in the ladies room showers at the Main street park, and walk up the street and over the bridge to the Bella Vista for a dinner of canned soup and grilled cheese. The walk was a half a mile. She loved crossing the gracefully curved North Bridge at sunset.

On Sunday of her first week in Robinson she took the bus to Mainland First Baptist. It was the church she went to every Sunday with the kids and Frank whenever they'd stayed at the beach house. There was a new pastor, Dr. Vance, and Ana decided to stay with Mainland right after that first sermon. He was young, and smart; Ana learned something she hadn't known that very first sermon. She loved learning new things. Dr. Vance taught that Jewish leaders in the time before Christ set up rules to protect the people from breaking the ten commandments which Dr. Vance called *fences*. What frightened the leaders about Christ was that, although he upheld the commandments, he tore down the fences. Ana had never heard that before and it intrigued her. She took the church bulletin back to the Inn, along with a list of needs from the table in the vestibule. Ana though long and hard about which jobs she felt she could do for the church. She decided on kitchen cleanup following the Wednesday and Sunday evening meals. She didn't want to cook, but she enjoyed a tidy kitchen. She also signed up to help with the teen girls' summer camp trip in late August, two weeks in the Keys right before school started. She dropped her membership and volunteer cards in the offering plate the following Wednesday at prayer meeting.

Although Ana thought of her time at the Inn as a vacation, and she allowed herself those long, lazy, sleepy afternoons in her personal beach cabana, she managed to set up her life and routine in Robinson with ease. She opened a post office box at the tiny beachside post office on Main Street, checking it every evening on her way back to the Inn. Ana had a habit of writing postcards. It was something her grandmother taught Ana to do when she was a child. Ana kept postcard stamps in her wallet, and a pen, and used blank postcards as book marks in her library books. Every evening except on Wednesday and Sunday she wrote a postcard. She'd been in the habit most of her life; her grandchildren kept their postcards. Children, Ana found, loved tradition.

So, in Ana's post office box she knew she would have an occasional postcard along with her bills. She also had a secret vice, a sometimes lucrative one, for which she needed the P.O. box: Ana loved to shop. What she really loved was a good bargain; she passed those bargains along on e-bay. Ana decided Wednesdays would be her shopping day. That way she could earn extra change on her debit card.

There was a store in town with two locations, one on the mainland out by the University, one on the beachside near the South Bridge, called Ringers Outlet. Ringers was a Florida chain of department stores which carried clothing and home goods. The outlets had a discount system where items were marked anywhere from twenty-five to ninety-five percent off using a series of colored dots. Wednesday was senior day. Shoppers over fifty years old received an additional discount of fifteen percent. Ana could theoretically purchase items at ninety-seven and a half percent off of the original price. The dots changed once a month, and items which for the previous month had been discounted to seventy-five percent moved to the ninety-five percent dot. Items weren't separated by discount in the stores. It took lots of time to go through the clearance rack to find things which were at maximum discount. It took a lot of experience to know what would sell on e-bay and what wouldn't. Ana went to the stores every Wednesday in search of the elusive ninety-seven and a half percent off items. Sometimes she was very lucky.

Ana didn't have wifi. She used her phone to take pictures, the computers at the University, and her post office box to conduct her e-bay business. She normally had only a couple of items up at a time and found that a three day auction made the most sense. Her first week in town she bought a lavender wool London Fog coat for $2.53. Ana sold it the following Saturday for $25 to a woman in Minnesota. The buyer paid shipping and Ana always used the free Priority Mail boxes at the post office, so the profit was over twenty one dollars after e-bay took their percentage. Ana loved the math of it, the guesswork on what would and would not sell, the strategizing.

Somehow all these careful, shallow activities kept Ana from thinking about the fact that she had no one. Oh, she had her children and grandchildren, and she saw them often enough, called them every Sunday. She talked to both her older sisters occasionally, and her two brothers. She had nothing at all to do with Frank's brother or sister. She had nobody in Robinson. When she got there that was what she wanted.

Ana remembered the first time she went into New York city alone. She'd taken a day for herself while Frank was working, taken the train in, wandered around. She took the ferry from Battery Park to Staten Island and back to look at the Statue of Liberty in the harbor. It was a freezing January day, she was a Florida girl; although she wore boots and a hat and gloves, a full-length wool coat, she still was unbelievably, unimaginably cold when she stood on the deck looking at Lady Liberty with the sun setting behind her. Inside, the ferry cabin seemed deliciously warm. She was just thawing out completely when the ferry docked at Battery Park. As Ana started down the long, curving, concrete ramp to the street she slipped on the smooth leather soles of her boots, sat, hard, on her bottom, and gained speed as she slid down the icy ramp all the way to the base. Ana held her hands out to her sides, keeping her balance all the way down. At the bottom, she was embarrassed for only a moment; two businessmen helped her to her feet, *are you okay, miss?* And moved quickly on at her brisk nod. Then she got tickled. Ana started laughing as she filled with a visceral, glorious freedom. She suddenly realized that, here, nobody had any idea who she was. In the city she was completely anonymous among the hundreds moving down the street. She could be anyone she wanted to be. She could slide all the way down the ferry ramp and not even bother to be embarrassed. She stood there on the street laughing until tears rolled down her cheeks. Nobody paid her any mind. It was wonderful.

Moving to Robinson was a conscious decision to slide down a ramp into a new, anonymous life. Before, Ana and her family had been "snowbirds," northerners who visited the rich end of the beach for holidays, vacations. Now she was a full-time resident and got to see what she wanted of the town. There are fewer individuals more invisible than a fifty-four year old widow, alone in the world.

All of this was in Ana's mind when she chose Robinson to come to. She didn't feel a deep connection to the town. But it served her purposes. She'd never gotten used to cold and snow and ice. She loved the sea, always had. The University with its generous senior citizen tuition-free policy gave her the sense that she was moving toward something. She chose social work as a major simply because it made sense—as far as Ana could tell, there were always jobs in that sector. She might need one someday, although she'd be the oldest novice social worker in history. Ana had not held a full-time job since working as a teenager. However, she had a lot of experience as a volunteer which served her well for her coursework.

By the time Ana checked out of the Bella Vista Inn, she was in full stride on her weekly schedule. She had slept later and later, stayed up into the wee hours to get used to her planned weekend nights volunteering in the emergency room. Soon she was a fixture there, except for when she had relatives in town, escorted the church teens to camp, or went out of town herself. On Friday and Saturday nights she didn't usually get to bed until around three, but managed to sleep in until 9:30 or 10:00; she still loved her afternoon naps—preferably after a long walk and swim at the beach—in her pop-up cabana on her air mat, a sea breeze ruffling and stirring the walls and mesh windows of the little tent.

Chapter 6

Ana realized that she had a decision to make even though she'd gained closure on Dr. Brewster's attempt to involve her in local issues and to single her out for her work in his class. Graduate school never occurred to Ana. At the pace she was going she'd get her bachelor's degree in two more years. That would make her nearly sixty. What was the point of graduate school at that age? Still, Ana did love studying, learning; it was one thing which made her feel connected to the world. Most of the time she felt wrapped in cotton, muffled. She liked it that way. For now. That's what she told herself, *for now*. But she'd always loved to read, and more and more that was what the coursework entailed. The study was getting more narrow and with that narrowness, that specificity, more interesting. And more challenging. She was managing to fill a lot of lonely hours in the school library working on her papers. Ana noticed that despite her advanced age she was not by any means the oldest student in her classes. There was some comfort—some strange, abstract comfort—in that. She wasn't the only geriatric out there looking to fill her days. And nights.

It became one more of Ana's secrets that she'd never told her children, grandchildren, or siblings she was in college. They thought she was leading the simple life of wealthy Florida widow. Ana wasn't sure how it had come to that, but little jokes were sometimes made about how Mom spends her time working on her tan and helping out those less fortunate with all that volunteer work. It was gentle, loving fun; but Ana was never certain exactly how to let everyone know what she was up to. She was wandering vaguely, but ever more specifically, toward a career. A late one, but a career nevertheless. Or at least a job. When she made family phone calls on Sundays Ana talked about the weather, about plans for upcoming trips or visits. She was adept at taking up conversational time asking her family about their own situations; school, work. Politics was a good safe area to discuss. Something was always happening, and both of her children were vocal liberals living in blue cities—purposefully so. This gave Ana a chance to listen and murmur ascent or questioningly at the right moments. Ana's school work never came up. As the semesters wore by she wasn't sure how to tell them. Maybe she would make it a stunning surprise by inviting them to commencement if she ever got to the point of graduation. Was it possible she was starting to plan beyond her next paper, or her next shift at the hospital?

When Ana walked or spent time at the beach—even among other bathers, not just when she was in her pop-up—she began to feel more separate from people, not less. When she passed the old black women on the causeway with their cane poles at dawn or dusk; when the kids on skateboards or bikes passed her on their way to work in the shops; when she worked in the library alongside Tiffany Sullivan, wife of the mayor or at the hospital near Judee, she began to feel more isolated than when she first moved to town. It wasn't that they were all different by skin color, social class, age. It was her secret. Ana had a secret which kept her apart from these others people.

When Ana finally stashed her book in her locker at the hospital— *The Goldfinch* was too fat to carry to the library in her already stuffed pack— she had trouble coming back into the present world. Tartt's characters seemed more real to her than people in her own life. The interiority. In the book, even the people who knew each other didn't know each other. Like real life. When Ana dealt with people—which she didn't feel she was good at and didn't particularly enjoy all that much—she tried to remember how little you got to know about a person. When Judee the Friday triage nurse was disdainful of uninsured patients, Ana tried to remember that Judee had an entire life and history which shaped her and Ana knew nothing of. Even with Frank, the person she she'd known best, right up until the end certain things surprised her, gave her the feeling there were things, important things, she would never know. Which of course was true.

When it became apparent Frank's illness was terminal and that the progress was going to be slow, Ana and Frank moved into a phase of life which became about only the two of them. And the medical staff, of course. Funny how you got to know nurses, techs; and how time in a hospital— later in a rehab, which was actually a place for dying—changed from the rhythms of ordinary life. Spending so much time there Ana actually began to *think* in a circular way which was a twenty-four hour period. Day and night ceased to be day and night in a more traditional way. Meals, lab work, doctor visits, shift changes—these were what drove time inside. That's how she thought about it, as inside. Going outdoors, anytime, was a shock to the system. Since Ana was allowed to be with Frank 24/7 in the last months, she developed the habit of being awake, reading or taking a walk around the grounds, in the wee hours of the morning. There were always people moving quietly about, soft lights on. Nurses on break leaving the grounds to smoke or stretch their legs.

The facility Frank was in was close to a river. There was a small park where Ana liked to sit and watch the water. She didn't much enjoy being home, then; the house became just a house without Frank in it; empty, echoing, sad. So she'd sit by the river and watch the water and wonder about the things underneath; fish, old bits of flotsam and jetsam, lost things, trash. She'd look at the smooth or rippling surface of the water and think the river was like a person, one thing on the outside and entirely something else within. She'd wondered what to do about Frank's family. He'd never told her much about them, really. She knew the basics but the most important thing was Frank wanted nothing to do with any of them. The only one he'd been close to was his mother, and they'd both worked at that, but she'd passed away years before. Ana didn't even know where his brother was. His sister was just plain scary. She was the kind of person who entered a room and controlled it in a sickly-sweet, passive-aggressive way. Anyone with a brain between their ears wouldn't dream of crossing her; you only had to know her for five minutes to see it wasn't worth it.

Frank had forgiven his family but not wanted to see them. They hadn't been told he was sick. Ana worried, a little, they would be angry with her for not getting in touch with them, but Frank was adamant. She never knew what his brother had done but it was telling—always had been—that Frank walked away from home at seventeen. The most he told Ana was (when she wondered at his lightning-fast acceptance of her own family when they were dating), "I walked away and they didn't even look for me. I lived under the boardwalk at the beach. I don't want to talk about it." They didn't.

Ana knew Frank's brother before she met Frank. She wanted to be friends, but Montgomery didn't. Everybody at school called him "Gome." He was one of the guys who hung around Ana's brother David. David was a grade ahead of Ana, and Gome a grade ahead of that. Sometimes he was at the house when Ana was in junior high. She always saw him with a book in his back pocket, which he'd whip out and read when the other guys were watching TV or working on surfboards or horsing around. She felt sorry for him; he obviously didn't fit with David's sharp-witted bunch, always a little late with a comment, and looked longingly at the girls who ran with the pack. Ana was accepted as David's little sister—the boys looked out for her at school and she felt safe around David's friends. Gome was the odd one out, so different from Frank that when she first met Frank she had a hard time believing they were brothers.

Frank was one of the best surfers Ana had ever seen, but he was reckless. He nearly got arrested several times for shooting the Flagler pier. Ana didn't know he was related to Gome, the boy she tried to befriend who kept her at a distance. She asked David once about Gome. He told her, "He's just a sad Catholic kid from up North. His mother runs that wine and cheese shop the snowbirds go to on the mainland, his dad's one of the carpetbaggers who doesn't understand what a beach town is, wants to sell as much of it as he can. He's got a little sister, thinks a lot of herself. She's a couple of years younger than you. And a brother who surfs, brown-haired guy with that hot-pink fish. Good surfer. I think Gome really has a thing for Laura Moxley. She works at his mom's shop, goes out with him once in a while. I don't care."

Laura and David had been flirting on and off since the sixth grade, dating in junior high but dating other people, too. That Gome had a crush on Laura made Ana feel sorrier for him; Laura was one of those bubbly girls who pretend to be good girls but are rotten to the core. David figured that out long ago, Ana knew.

There was something off about Gome. Ana never figured out what it was but she guessed not long into her marriage to Frank it might have something to do with why he left home so young, and so abruptly.

Ana wasn't sure why the novel made her think of all that, so long ago. Death, she supposed. All three of the Donna Tartt books Ana read started with death. That was something she understood. Ana walked down Sycamore Street from the hospital the five residential blocks to the library. The street was beautiful; three blocks west of the river, live oaks as old as the town itself arced over the narrow road and their roots made the sidewalk tricky to navigate. The houses were old too, nothing like the concrete block structures, built to survive hurricanes, on the beachside and causeways. These were elegant as old ladies dressed up for tea at a Junior League meeting. Their windows were beautiful, casement and paladin, shutters painted to match the trim on the clay and slate roofs. Most were two-storied. A few had basements. The yards were shaded by oaks and magnolia trees, littered with leaves and moss and twigs, and the walks curving to wide porches strolled among the trees as if time were something to be dealt with not at all.

This was not a street Ana would walk at night. Not because it wasn't a good neighborhood; it was the best in town. But the sidewalks needed to be replaced. She knew why they weren't: killing the roots of a live oak killed the tree. Sometimes Ana walked in the street, because it was easier and there was little traffic. Most people used either Riverside Drive or the Dixie Freeway, U.S. 1, two blocks west.

The library was fairly new, a sprawling, square, one-story building set at an angle so the front door was in one of the corners. It occupied a space between Sycamore and U.S. 1, two blocks, with wide lawns and no trees. The door faced Sycamore. Ana worked two hours a week, and she didn't have to do a lot with other volunteers. Her job was to take books dropped in the book return over the last couple of days, scan them with a hand scanner, and put them on carts for different sections of the library for other workers to shelve. Simple. Unfortunately her work space—a desk against the wall with space for her to wheel the big canvas basket of books next to—was within conversational distance of the volunteer break area. Most of the volunteers who'd made overtures of friendship toward Ana had gotten the idea over the past few years that she wasn't communicative. They knew Ana liked to be alone. She wasn't the only shy person—customer, staff, or volunteer—who sought peace and quiet at the library. She was friendly enough and always kind; she just didn't gossip or joke. She worked quietly by herself.

Tiffany Sullivan was the wife of one of the developers who'd moved over from Orlando. She was a Robinson native—her father was a realtor and so was Tiffany. She had short, short blond hair, big brown eyes, and what Frank had called, "after-market bolt-ons"; fake breasts. Tiffany never seemed to understand Ana liked to work without distraction. She wasn't in the break room or library often; she was in charge of the volunteers but always rushing to one place or another, her starched button down shirts and skinny jeans impeccable no matter what. Ana managed to hide her disappointment at Tiffany's presence as she wheeled the return cart next to the desk.

"Hi Ana!" Tiffany crooned, "How's it going? I'm grabbing a Tab. Do you remember Tab? I'm just addicted. I special order them. Have been drinking them since high school. Anyway, I keep some here in the fridge, if you ever want one. Do you want one?"

For some strange reason, despite her Lexus visible through the window, her perfect hair and face, Ana felt sorry for Tiffany today. She sat down at the break table instead of the desk. "Sure."

"Great!" Tiffany popped up like a Donna Tartt character living on amphetamines and diet soda. She got another Tab from the fridge and set it down with a thump in front of Ana. "Oops! Give that a minute! Actually I wanted to talk to you. I wanted to ask where you got that amazing basic black you wore to the library dinner. You always look so, I don't know, simple and chic at the same time."

Ana smiled. "I've had that dress forever. I can't remember where I got it. New York, I think. I shopped there sometimes when we lived in Jersey." Why was Ana telling somebody like Tiffany this? She couldn't remember the last person she told she'd lived in New Jersey.

"Oh, I go up a couple of times a year for shows! Maybe we could go together sometime. I go in October, and then in May. New York is wonderful in spring, but you have to be really careful not to get the front edge of summer. It stinks in summer."

"Well, I should get to work. Thanks for the drink."

"Oh sure." Tiffany made a face. "I need to get out there anyway. I'm relieving Janna in the computer section. I hate working there. All those smelly homeless people who come in! And you have to take the time to help them with the one-time use pass. There ought to be an easier way. Or a rule. Maybe we can get rid of the one-time use passes. But, that might be rough on the snowbirds who are here less than half the year. And of course on the tourists. Oh, well. You're lucky you work back here."

"Actually, I send some of the homeless people here. Sorry. It's really the only place in town for public computer access, and sometimes we get people at the emergency room who need to fill out online forms for Medicaid."

"Ana," Tiffany drawled as she opened the door to the break room, "I don't know how you find the time. I mean, I know you're retired and all, and young I might add! But I see you volunteering all over the place. You are a walking wonder."

When Tiffany was gone Ana turned to the desk, got the hand held scanner out of a lower drawer, stacked the books from the bin onto the desk, and got to work. She felt funny, and realized what she felt was lonely. She put the scanner down. How could chatting with Tiffany Anderson and drinking a Tab make her lonely? Tiffany had to be one of the shallowest people she'd met. She reminded Ana of her absolutely depthless sister-in-law, Midgie. Midgie believed everything. She believed God wasn't in us, God was us. We were God. The table was God, the telephone pole was God, the duct tape was God, the long-life battery, the ace bandage, the dog shit on the bottom of your shoe. It had driven Frank right up the wall, he swore she had always been that way. From birth. Midgie decided when she was a little girl she wouldn't marry anyone who couldn't raise her station—she was not going to stay the shopkeeper and realtor's daughter. She would marry up. And she did. She married a lawyer's son who became a lawyer himself, in fact in Orlando; Ana saw him on billboards every time she took her grandkids to the airport. They had to add extra billboard space for Lester's big, bald forehead. *Hurt at work? Slip and fall in the market? Lester Lister, he's your man!*

Midgie didn't stop at marrying up. She'd also decided to go through college, and had a master's degree in paranormal psychology. She and Lester adopted two little girls from China in the 1990s because she didn't want to ruin her figure or her sex life with childbirth. When Midgie found out Frank was sick, she traveled to Jersey and came to the rehab center. She claimed if he did yoga daily for one hour in a room at 105 degrees, he'd live. Frank pretended to be asleep when she came again, and after Ana told her, "No" when she insisted Ana wake him, his sister left in a huff. That was one of the last laughs she'd shared with her husband; laughing their asses off at his ridiculous sister.

So why did Ana feel lonely after Tiffany left? She looked, and acted, a lot like Midgie. Except Tiffany had a small nose and Midgie a ski-slope. Midgie never annoyed Ana as much as she did Frank. At least she was honest about her ambitions; what she wanted was money, and she didn't mind deliberately marrying to get it. Tiffany seemed to have some of that same drive; but from what Ana could tell, she made her own money and plenty of it. Maybe that was the similarity, the money. She shouldn't sell Tiffany short, attributing Midgie's shallowness to her just because they looked alike and both had money. Maybe she could go on a theater trip with her, if she really meant it and asked again.

What was she thinking? A theater trip? With a hyper woman she didn't even know? She might end up in a yoga class—oh how Frank had despised trends!—or an ashram.

As Ana was signing out at the time clock Tiffany came back through the break room. "Bye, Ana, it was great chatting with you! I sometimes see you out on the beach down in Haven. We must live in the same neighborhood. We really should get together some time. Take that theater trip! You could show me the real New York! Here. Take a Tab for the road."

Tiffany set another Tab on the table with another thump, snapped her timecard through the slot and whirled out of the room, designer bag swinging behind her. Ana left her own things and went out to the stacks to find a book. Volunteers got to keep library books as long as they wanted to but Ana found she finished most within a week. However, she liked to read more than one book at a time. Today she headed straight for fiction to the Ms. She knew what she wanted. When she was really down nothing brought her out of it like Travis McGee. There were only a couple of dozen books in the series. Ana saved them up for when she was really low. When Frank was sick, she couldn't get through any one book; novels couldn't hold her.

The books, by John D. MacDonald, didn't have to be read in order. Sometimes Ana even read them over. She had a few she was saving up for the future—unread. Today, she checked out *The Empty Copper Sea.* She'd read it before, years ago, but it was one of her favorites. MacDonald's descriptions of Florida, even ones written decades ago, were spot-on. He captured the corruption and the beauty, the rape of the land and water, and the untamable wildness of the state; the transience of the people and the permanence of locals. All the sleaze; all the variability and storms and fecundity. The fresh smell of the ocean after a hard rain.

Ana went back to the break room, picked up her pack and her new Tab and a couple of mini-muffins from a Tupperware container on the table, left the library and walked down seventh to Riverside Drive. There was a park underneath the only high-rise bridge in town, the south bridge, where fishing was good and docks jutted from shore in the shade of the bridge span. Ana liked to sit in the shade of a rough-barked juniper between the duck pond and the children's playground. By the time it was getting too dark to read, she was three chapters in and her loneliness a thing of the past.

Chapter 7

The next evening Ana felt restless during prayer meeting and went back to the kitchen to make sure everything was ready for the meal. All the food was laid out, but there were pots and pans she could scrub. She'd stayed for the songs and prayer requests at the beginning of service; there were close to a hundred people in the congregation. She slipped out during the prayer right before the sermon began. There was a speaker in the kitchen. Ana could listen to the sermon as she did the dishes.

Ana loved washing dishes. All of her brothers and sisters did, too. When they were growing up washing dishes was at the top of the chore hierarchy. Their father usually got to do the dishes—an engineer, he love doing things precisely and well. He passed that to his children. He folded clothes, made beds, washed dishes, swept floors, changed diapers. Both of Ana's parents enjoyed housework, but everyone enjoyed washing dishes. All her life, if something was bothering Ana she calmed down putting her hands in hot, soapy water and making things clean. She filled the deepest sink a third of the way with hot, soapy water and got to work, tuning her mind to the words coming over the speaker.

The sermon this evening was on loving your enemy. "I saw a bumper sticker the other day," the pastor said, "which read, *When Jesus said love your enemy, I'm pretty sure he meant 'don't kill them.'* What do you think about that? Do you think it is possible to love your enemy, and to kill them? Did Jesus tell us to love them? Well, of course he did. But what does that mean, to love? Is it a verb for you, or a noun? Does love involve action? I believe so. We are also told to 'bless them that curse you, do good to them that hate you, and pray for them that despitefully use you, and persecute you' Matthew 5:44.

"I am here to tell you, none of that is easy. What would be easy is to tell ourselves, *that's a goal.* We are to strive to be Christ-like, and Christ is perfect, and we can't be perfect. That's a cop out! You could do all this—

love your enemies, pray for them that use and persecute you, do good for those who hate you, and bless those who curse you, and you'd still be far from perfect. It's not a goal. It is a living, breathing, day to day *expectation* from your Lord to you, as a Christian. We don't have a choice about this. It is what we are to do. Love is action: loving your enemy involves prayer. It involves *doing* good.

"Another thing to consider: what makes an enemy? It isn't always a two-way street, is it? You may have enemies in people who despise *you,* even if you love them. They are still, by definition, your enemy if they have done that. You have to do good for them. That's difficult. I want us all to think about an enemy, and pray for that enemy this week. Let's be honest— we all have them. And, let's think about that bumper sticker. That's one of the harder things. A lot of Christians in this nation use their faith in a very bad way; to judge and to fear. Two things we are commanded not to do. I'm not telling you how to vote or what political party to belong to. But if your politics involve killing your enemy? If your politics involve pointing your fingers at fellow citizens and judging their choices, you need to get new politics if you call yourself a Christian. 'Judge not, that ye be not judged.' Matthew 7:1"

Okay, enemies. Ana couldn't think of a single person she hated. She thought that perhaps Frank had hated his siblings—but he'd never actually said so. She certainly didn't hate them. Ana tried to think about anyone who hated her. That would be hard to know, she'd never really had trouble getting along with anyone, even as a child. But there were some people she held strong anger toward, and she'd just been thinking about them today. Midgie was one. When Ana and Frank had been married four years, Midgie went to Robin's daycare center, picked him up, and got on a plane with Lester to Paris. She called Frank and said she had decided Robin would have a better life with her and Lester, and he was such a cute little boy; since Ana had already ruined her body with one birth, she could have more. Midgie would take this one.

Ana was completely sideswiped by the kidnapping. The woman was clearly crazy but she also had Ana's child. Just because she wanted him for her own didn't mean she would not harm Robin. Ana called her brothers. She and Frank, David and Russ flew to France. It took two weeks and every penny they had to get the baby back. Ana and Frank fought bitterly about it; she wanted to press charges. He didn't. After a month Ana moved with Robin into her own apartment and took a job at an elementary school as a teaching assistant. It was two years before she and Frank worked things out enough to get back together, but Ana hated Midgie for a long time after that. An enemy? No, not really. Ana mostly felt sorry for her—she was clearly nuts. Pray for her? That was difficult. She wondered if Frank had been wrong or right about staying away from Gome and Midgie. Just smart? They had, as a couple, prayed for Frank's family all the time. But Frank still preferred not to see his brother or his sister. His mother died two years before Frank, and he had spent quite a bit of time with her in her final years. She, too, had very little to do with her other children. She'd lost his father to cancer ten years before and lived alone in Maryland for the last years of her life. Ana and Frank drove down for holidays, or Sarah drove up; she was close to both Robin and Ella. A good grandma, she remembered their birthdays and loved to spend time with them. But Ana had been afraid, always, when the children were young that Midgie would show up again. After she'd heard about Midgie and Lester going to China and adopting, she thought she should feel safer, but she didn't.

Midgie lived in Orlando. Ana wondered that if Midgie really was her enemy, she'd need to see her. She hoped not. It might be something she could consult with Dr. Vance about. First she needed to pray for her. Ana never considered letting Midgie and Lester know she was here. They lived in Winter Park, a town Frank said should have the motto *An Ounce of Pretension is Worth a Pound of Manure.* How somebody as down to earth as Frank could have a sister like Midgie was a mystery. Ana decided she could pray for Midgie, but would have to think long and hard about how she could do good for her. After all, she didn't know if Midgie hated her or not. She didn't want to know.

Ana finished tidying the big church kitchen by the time the serving crew came in for the meal—macaroni and cheese, salad, biscuits, and baked chicken—and took it into the fellowship hall. About half of the congregation stayed to eat on Wednesdays. Ana wouldn't be needed for cleanup again until after everyone had eaten, so she sat down to enjoy her meal. When the pastor gave the blessing, Ana silently added, "Lord, please....bless...Midgie...and Lester." Even though she offered the prayer only in her mind and heart, Ana noticed her teeth were clenched. So were her fists.

Ana got to the University before noon the next day. She didn't want to take a chance of Dr. Brewster seeing her at the bus stop. She knew he had office hours Thursday afternoon, so she avoided the social sciences building and went straight to the library. She thought she was in pretty good shape for her geology final that evening but she wanted to study. She found a comfortable chair up on the quiet floor, in the back behind the stacks near the rare books room, and took out her notes.

Ana was surprised how much she liked the geology class. She'd had no idea the surface of the earth, and how it came to be, could be so interesting. She had traveled a good bit and saw a lot of geological formations on train trips, but learning things like Mohs Hardness Scale and about Karst topography came easily to Ana because she enjoyed it. She glanced through her notes, set her wristwatch alarm, and spent a few peaceful hours before class with Travis MaGee.

When Ana was a teenager, and got in trouble a few times—coming in late and making a D in calculus—her parents sent her to stay with her brothers in Tallahassee. Russ lived in Wakulla, half an hour from town. He drove in to classes in his pickup truck. David lived close to campus. Ana loved being sent to Tallahassee; it was the seventies, and a fun town. Russ belonged to the co-op; it was a *true* co-op. He brought strawberries and okra from his garden, worked a few hours a week, and got points to buy food. Even though Ana was only fourteen the first time she was sent to Tally, she was allowed to help out at the co-op, too. It felt good to earn her food. She'd work in the back or in the aisles while Russ cashiered. Ana loved the way the place smelled; fresh vegetables and rain on dusty earth. The floor was concrete and took a lot of sweeping, but it held the smell of Florida on a hot afternoon. There was a deli counter with cheeses Ana never tried before: Havarti, Munster. The breads were rich, dark things—a slice of bread with cheese made a meal. She tried new things. At home Ana avoided vegetables, but in Tallahassee she ate bean sprouts and tomatoes.

After working an hour or two Russ drove them to campus. Ana could go to classes with him or wander around; nobody seemed to mind. Sometimes she slipped into the back of the larger classes to listen to lectures. Once a girl, a hippie like Russ and David, came up to her when Ana was sitting outside the union, "Excuse me, but I have to tell you, you look just like my boyfriend's friend, Rusty Mills." That knocked Ana out.

After Russ got out of class they usually headed over to a friend's house in town, or sometimes drove straight back to Wakulla to hang out with friends there. Twice they stayed in town to listen to bluegrass and folk music on the green at the University. On weekends, Ana's brothers and their friends took her swimming in sinkholes out in the country. They were beautiful, back in the woods on private land, but Russ was so friendly the people who owned the land let him swim there. He told her sinkholes were very deep, fed by an underground river. The water felt icy cold. The best way to get in was just to jump right in. Some of the kids swam naked, but Ana was shy and always wore a bathing suit, and sometimes a t-shirt and shorts against the cold.

The sinkholes were holes in the ground filled with water. Most of them had steep sides of limestone. Trees, oaks and pines, crowded the edges and usually someone had hung a stout rope from an oak limb. Because the sides of the holes were so steep, it was safe to swing out and drop. Then you'd swim, deep if you wanted to, and watch the others swing and laugh and when you got tired, climb carefully up the easiest side to navigate and find a sunny spot to warm up. After swimming Ana was always tired, but it was a good tired. Back home in Flagler after a day in the water she always said she was *beached out*. This was the same sort of feeling, only instead of itchy from salt and sun her skin felt clean, the cleanest it ever was. The water was marvelous. Ana was a swimmer since almost before she could walk. She felt at home in the water—all the Mills did. It was something their mother insisted on, learning to swim very young, if they were going to be raised near the ocean.

Now, studying Karst topography brought Ana back to those Tallahassee days. She wished she could tell Russ and David about her class. Something held her back. Still, she promised herself she'd call Russ and chat with him this weekend, see if he remembered taking her to Tallahassee when she was a kid. He'd met his wife, Daisy, after Ana's first exile to Tally; she had been a part of Ana's life ever since. Ana liked Daisy, who was a botanist. The way she talked about plants it was almost as if they had personalities: what they liked, how they could be controlled, why they behaved in certain ways.

Ana was one of the last students in class to finish her final. It hadn't been particularly difficult and she felt she did well, but she usually went over every question a couple of times on a test to be sure she hadn't mixed anything up or missed something. One of the things she learned about herself by going to college was that she was not a procrastinator. This surprised Ana. She'd always felt behind, before; now she was organized and prepared. She usually did her assignments and readings the night they were assigned, reviewing them before they were due. Sometimes, if the syllabi allowed her to work ahead, Ana did. But not too. She didn't want to appear over-eager or get so far ahead she forgot what she had studied when the lecture for that topic came up. Ana planned her papers out so they were finished well ahead, and studied for her finals for weeks instead of cramming. She was too old for that; her brain and body didn't work that way. Ana often saw young students drinking energy drinks and sweating late into the night in the study center and the library during reading week. She felt sorry for them, but since she had never been a college student as a young woman, she didn't have any idea what that was like.

Ana walked over to the library after class and wrote a couple of post cards. She wrote one to her granddaughter Elise, who was going to be starting her senior year of high school next month. Ana had some Dr. Seuss postcards. She chose one which read *Oh, the places you'll go!*

Dear Elise,

> *I hope you are ready for senior year to start. I was just thinking about how, when I was your age, my parents used to send me up to Tallahassee to stay with my brothers sometimes, and what a terrific time I always had with them. Your mother told me you are interested in Florida State. If you go there I can show you some fantastic places—sinkholes you can swim in—I'm sure they are still there! And, just think, Casey can come stay with you just like I stayed with Uncle Russ and Uncle Dave!*
>
> > *Hugs,*
> > *Grandma Ana*

Her second card was to her sister Mary who lived in Newtown, Connecticut.

Dear Mary,

> *How are you? Cooler than I am, I'll bet. Florida summers can be brutal, as I'm sure you recall from our childhood—but at least every building in town has air conditioning these days, I don't know how we did it! Remember taking all our beds out to the Florida room, lining them up in a row, and opening the jalousies to catch ANY breeze off the ocean? And how we had to keep whisk brooms by our beds to keep the sand out? Ah, well. Progress, thy name is A.C. I just wanted to send you this card—I saw it the other day and thought of you. Call me one of these days and let me know what's up, up there,*
>
> > *Love,*
> > *Ana*

Mary's card had a picture of two little girls, shot from behind, holding a giant, old-fashioned yellow and blue canvas raft by its ropes as they raced toward the Atlantic at Haven Beach. Ana and Mary used to share a raft rented from a beach concession when they were small. Beach concessions did brisk business at Haven all summer. Ana'd picked up the card at one of the surf shops on A.1.A.

Ana always felt a little strange at the end of a semester. It was remarkable how rapidly they were going by. Dr. Brewster's casual assumption Ana would be continuing school after she graduation itched at her. Maybe next week before she chaperoned the church girls at camp she'd look into it. Something she'd discovered about college puzzled Ana. It was easier than high school. As a mother, and a grandmother, Ana had learned a few things about children. For example, over time children don't change. An eight year old is an eight year old is an eight year old; a seventeen year old is a seventeen year old; 1974, or 1997, or 2015. She'd always thought it ridiculous when she was a child and more so now, when adults complained about *kids these days*. It wasn't the kids which changed, it was the days. What children were exposed to, what was expected of them. The times. Ana saw the incredulity, the incomprehension on her grandchildren's faces when she told them about back in the day (just as she was astonished at the conditions in her own grandmother's olden days); that there was one television in a home and it got four channels at best. No such thing as video, no way to record a show, and no such thing as even reruns. That telephones all were hard-wired into the wall, and when you called somebody you got one of three things on the other end of the line: a live human being, a busy signal, or endless rings. No such thing as voicemail or answering machines.

Ana's only experiences as a young person with college had been wandering around F.S.U. while her brothers were in class, in the hippie days. Compared to then, everything seemed fast and tense now at the University of East Florida. Still, she'd had an inkling then of what she now knew to be true: college was easier than high school. She wondered if grad school would be easier than undergrad—certainly her upper level classes were easier than general education ones. This, she knew, was because the material was more interesting. Ana was able to take most of her classes in what fascinated her, which was her major: social work. And, for the few electives she had left, she picked things she actually wanted to know about. The required lower level classes had sometimes been uninteresting, which made them more difficult. It was easy to see why high school was harder: seven rigorous classes, actually being *in* class more than thirty five hours weekly. In college the most time Ana spent in class was six hours per week, and that was half-time; even if she were going full-time she'd be spending twenty-three hours less time in school than a high school student. Pretty easy to see why education got easier as you moved above high school.

Chapter 9

After every semester Ana celebrated in some small way. She'd skipped her Ringer's shopping and e-baying this week so she had nothing to mail out, nothing for sale online. But, she did have a little money to play with and thought this weekend she might pick up a new bathing suit and a less formal all-purpose dress for her trip with the church girls to the Keys. They were going to have two days away from the camp ground at John Pennekamp, the only underwater National Park, and Ana was looking forward to it. As a child she sailed catamarans. She planned to teach the girls and the other chaperones a thing or two on the water.

One of her biggest regrets resulted from something which happened on a cat boat. She'd spent the summer she was sixteen working nights at a local Italian Restaurant, and days on the beach by herself. That was unusual. Her mother always required the children to go anywhere, particularly to the beach, in pairs. But she was away for the summer taking care of her own mother who was ill, and Ana was feeling her age. Everybody else in the family was away—at least during the day—and she spent the summer mostly alone. There were young men on the beach who had cat boats. Ana saw girls, mostly older girls, go up in pairs and small groups giggling, to talk the boys into taking them out on the boats. It was obviously a social dance of some kind. Ana watched for weeks.

One day in July she approached a tall, thin, twenty-something guy with a 16' Prindle with a striped yellow and white sail. "Will you take me out?" Ana blurted.

The man looked a little startled. He had brown eyes and hair, a ragged Hang-Ten t-shirt, and Sundek baggies. "Uh, sure. I'm Dale. What's your name? How old are you?"

"I'm Ana Therill. I'm....only sixteen. But I'm really good on the water, I can surf, and I grew up here. I really want to learn to sail."

Surprisingly, the man's frown disappeared. "Therill? You related to

Russ and Dave? I love those guys. Heard they went up to FSU. Smart fellas."

"They're my brothers. So will you teach me?"

"Sure, happy to. They coming home this summer?"

Just like that, Ana slipped into the role she'd enjoyed among her brothers' friends when she was younger. She and Dale went out on the boat two or three times a week. She got the hang of sailing quickly. Ana's best subject in school last year had been physics, and she loved applying the laws of physics to the art of sailing. She liked Dale. He made her feel less lonely for her brothers and sisters. Dale had a lawn-care business and stayed burnt brown on his arms, legs, and face. But Ana was very young, and didn't realize that what felt like a sibling relationship to her could be perceived as something else by Dale.

Ana had started dating Frank and hadn't yet told him about her sailing excursions. He worked as a lifeguard a couple of miles up the beach; Ana and Dale always sailed south. One afternoon, after a particularly trying journey back up the beach tacking into a strong breeze, Dale let the sail luff so they could rest a half a mile out before running in. He was quieter than usual today, and Ana was anxious to get in to the beach to clean up. She had the night off. She and Frank were planning to run down to Ormond Beach to watch a surf movie at the theater there.

"Ana," said Dale. And stopped. "Ana." Even under his tan Ana could see him reddening. She wondered what was wrong. He was looking down at his hands, wrapping and rewrapping his left one nervously in the sheet. "How about you marry me? We have a lot of fun together. I've got a good job. Let's get married."

Ana stared at him. Open-mouthed. Then, she couldn't help it, she laughed. "Dale! Oh, my goodness, you are so funny!"

Dale looked off toward the beach, "Yeah. Let's go in." Ana followed his eyes. Frank was standing at the end of the pier, waving his arms. "Do you know that guy?"

"Sure! That's my friend Frank! We're going to the movies. Want to come with us?"

"Nah. I'm…..tired."

Dale was quiet all the way in. Ana hopped off the tramp as soon as they hit the beach. "See you, Dale! Thanks!"

She never saw Dale again. It was years before Ana realized he wasn't joking, that she'd probably hurt him. She told Frank about it after Robin was born. They were talking about how beautiful he was. "Thank God he looks like you," Ana said. "I was afraid he'd look like me. I still don't know why you married me. I never thought I'd get married, I thought I'd be an old maid." Frank smiled. "That guy? You remember that guy who taught me to sail when we were kids? You saw him once. That day, out on the water, he asked me to marry him. He'd never kissed me! Never taken me out on a date! It was nice of him to joke around, though, that I might get a husband some day."

"Ana," said Frank, "what on earth made you think he was joking?"

Years later, with a few more social fumbles under her belt it occurred to Ana that she'd been thoughtless, even cruel. There were men out there who didn't care about skin-deep beauty. Or, ugliness.

On Friday Ana called the church to make sure there were plenty of people to hand out food from the pantry to the needy for Free Bread Friday. Today Ana was treating herself to celebrate the end of her seventh successful semester. She picked up a turkey, bacon, and provolone sub with mayo, salt, pepper, and lettuce at the French Bakery on the South Causeway and a large bottle of mineral water. Ana usually just refilled her BPA-free bottle with tap water. She bought a napoleon, too. She found a quiet spot at the south end of Haven Beach, set up her pop-up shelter, stashed her backpack and lunch, and peeled off her t-shirt and sweat pants. Ana didn't need to put on sunscreen; she put it on every morning of her life, first thing. Ana started protecting her skin as a teen long before it became the thing to do. Now she was glad. When her girlfriends were still melting sticks of butter and mixing it with a couple of drops of iodine, rubbing it on and basically cooking in the hot Florida sun, Ana wore long sleeves and cotton pants to walk on the beach, with a floppy hat and sun glasses. She'd even used a little screen room at the beach and stayed in the shade way back then. Although she had her father's reddish-brown, Native American skin tone—and rarely burned even when she used to tan—Ana felt, very young, that skin care was important. Every day after the beach as a teenager Ana broke pieces off the aloe plant by the front door and rubbed the juice on her skin.

As a result of all the care she gave it, Ana's skin was beautiful. Because her diet included lots of water and lots of fruit and vegetables, her skin looked much younger than other people's her age, especially other Floridians. Up north she noticed people had skin so white it was almost luminous. Ana also noticed that the longer a person smoked, the worse the effect on the skin. Midgie smoked. No amount of expensive creams or cosmetics could hide that—Ana noticed how old she looked when she'd come to Jersey to see Frank in the rehab.

Ana zipped up her shelter and walked down the beach to the water. She planned to spend the whole day at the beach, which was unusual because she normally had something scheduled every day of the week. Today the tide was low in the morning and the water unusually clear. It was warm as bathwater. She could see her feet clearly as she stood in the shorebreak to check the sea as she'd learned to do, long ago. The lifeguard was on her tower a hundred yards to the north, and there were a couple of surfers catching the morning glass. The outside break, beyond the sandbar, was beautiful; little two to three foot peaks. A gentle off-shore breeze kept the surf clean. Perfect longboard waves. She saw a young couple out at the sandbar in front of the guard working with their little boy.

Down toward the national seashore, Ana could see five people walking slowly, looking for shells, and one man with a metal detector. Low tide in the morning was the perfect time for shelling. Her's was the only sun shelter, but she knew by the end of the afternoon there would be half a dozen or so along this stretch of beach. They were good not only for privacy and sun protection, but as shelter from the occasional hard downpour if it wasn't accompanied by lightning. One of Ana's earliest childhood lessons was to take solid shelter at even the hint of lightning. Today was going to be clear. The sun already shown white above the horizon, and as she looked at the sea she could tell there were no runouts, the visible signs of rip currents. Ana had been caught in rips a few times, and simply *took the escalator out*, as the locals said, then swam parallel to shore until she could swim in. It was scary, but not too dangerous as long as the swimmer stayed calm. Every year at least one tourist drowned in a rip. The lifeguards were good here, though: Ana tried to stay close enough to one to get help if she needed it.

As soon as she finished checking out the water, Ana waded in and body surfed for twenty minutes. Even though it was early she went in and ate lunch. It wouldn't do to get food poisoning when she had such a peaceful day planned. After, she went up to the restrooms, threw away her trash, and took a quick shower. Today and through the weekend Ana planned to *get a little color,* as her mother used to say. She would be outside more than usual during the day in the Keys and wanted to establish just a touch of tan as skin protection against that stronger light. She went back to her shelter, opened the windows and the wide door, and settled down with *The Empty Copper Sea,* feeling relaxed and satiated and blessed to be living in one of the prettiest towns on the planet.

That evening after her shift at the hospital, Ana wrote a note for the other volunteers and tucked the corner of it under the Tupperware container in the middle of the table, which held an assortment of goodies people brought in over the last few days. There was always some sweet inside. Tonight it contained Toll House cookies and Jennifer Winters' lemon toffee bars, which Ana was partial to. She resisted them as she set the container on the edge of the note:

Hello all,

Just letting you know, I'll be away for the next two weeks, so won't be able to do uniforms. Will try to bring back some key limes!
Ana
8-14-2015

She also wrote **Ana away** on the large white board calendar on the wall next to the refrigerator, and drew a line through the next three weeks since she wouldn't return to her volunteer job at the hospital until the evening of September 4th. The calendar served as time card for the volunteers. It was a smart way for those who missed her note to be reminded to handle their own uniforms for the next three weeks.

On Saturday Ana shopped for the trip and packed. She would leave her pack at the church Sunday morning after service since they'd be taking the church bus bright and early on Monday. She'd found a beautiful chocolate-brown swimsuit at Ringers Outlet in her size, an 8, so she had that and her old swimsuit. She'd found not one but two wrinkle-free dresses which would be perfect for evening chapel at the camp; one a sleeveless blue the color of the Atlantic on a clear day at noon past the outside break. The other was a paisley print with high waist and long, floaty skirt which dropped almost to her feet, and sheer ¾ sleeves. Both were of that new material which was light as a feather, and both had underlining which made slips unnecessary. They billowed out from the body instead of hugging it, for comfort. Progress. Ana was a fan.

She packed all three dresses and her black ballet flats (in a Ziploc bag) in the very bottom of her pack. Her swimsuits and sunscreen went together in another bag in one of the side pockets; wallet, sunglasses, telephone, and headphones in the other. Ana was taking another Travis McGee novel and, because she couldn't put it down and couldn't imagine two weeks without the story, *The Goldfinch*. She had a lightweight King James

Bible covered in bright green leather she'd picked up years ago. Those three books, along with a pen and highlighter (Ana used the highlighter in her Bible during services or when she found something she needed to remind herself of during study) went in the front pocket. In the main compartment of her pack, on top of her dresses and flats, Ana placed three pair of white panties and three bras. All of her clothes, except the no-wrinkle dresses, she rolled instead of folding as she was taught as a child to do when traveling. She took three t-shirts; a pair of long twill shorts and one of lightweight linen slacks; one button-down in a buttery yellow cotton, and a forest green nylon warm-up suit. On top of that, a sleeveless cotton night gown and her zippered toiletry kit with the handy hook and mesh pockets—it could hang from a shower or closet bar in open or closed position to be aired out or allow things to dry. In it were her tooth brush, toothpaste, deodorant, travel-size bodywash and shampoo, a comb, a tiny first aid kit containing: bandages, sample-sized aspirin and pain-reliever and antibiotic packets, a small ace bandage, and tweezers. With it zipped almost closed, Ana slipped in a small box of three individual packets of powdered laundry detergent. She would do her laundry every three days. From experience she knew she would be teased a little about how lightly she packed: one bag only. But Ana loved to travel light. She stuffed three pair of crew socks down beside her clothes, and topped it all with an empty, folded and zipped-up bright red bag which was the library's gift to volunteers last year; it folded out from the size of a thin paperback book to a full-sized, waterproof bag for carrying books and contained an ingenious clear plastic rain poncho. On the outside was stenciled Ana's name in white, with *thank-you for all you do for Robinson Public Library, 2014*. Ana would use the bag for her gear when at the beach. She'd purchase a cheap pair of flip-flops in the Keys, and towels were provided at the camp. Since she only snorkeled once a year— on this trip—Ana simply left her snorkel, mask, and fins, with her name in black Sharpie on each, in the gear bin at the youth house. She knew that when the boys went in June somebody might use her equipment, but it didn't matter: she'd soak her gear overnight in the tub in her cabin with a few drops of bleach before using it again.

Her pack when Ana hefted it was uncomfortably heavy; she wondered if she should break her personal rule and use a suitcase instead. Then she remembered *The Goldfinch*. It was a hardcover, and hundreds of pages—a hefty book. Ana set the pack, which had a sturdy leather bottom, on the table and unzipped the front pocket, took out the book, and slipped the pack on. Ahh, much better. That was comfortable. She slipped it off and stood it up on the table again. She shook the pack by its handle to shift everything in the main compartments around, taking up the space in the front pocket where the book had been by compressing it forward. Ana wasn't willing to leave the book; she would simply carry it. She planned to read on the bus all the way down, anyway; her job on this trip wasn't to supervise the teens, of which there were a dozen this year, but to be available as a grandma-figure in the evenings if any of the chaperones or girls had concerns they wanted to share with someone who wasn't one of the moms. Three mothers were going. They would stay in the separate bedroom attached to the girls' bunk-room. Ana's cabin was a hundred yards from the bunkhouse, closer to the Atlantic shore. She was looking forward to all the privacy and time to read at the camp, and not worried about finishing her books. There was a small library in the cabin. She'd simply carry her fat novel onto the bus, read all the way down if she felt like it; she liked to put on her headphones, which were foldable, over-the-ear, soft ones; tuck the wire into her pack, and read undisturbed. When she was reading, Ana couldn't hear anything; the rumble of the bus and the chatter of its occupants would fade and Ana be transported right into the author's imagined world.

Ana realized she had forgotten two things: her inflatable pillow, and her sun shelter. The shelter slipped easily into the straps on the inside of the pack, meant she believed for a skateboard. In the interest of not appearing standoffish, Ana wouldn't take it with her. The camp provided easy-ups and chairs. She did, however, want to take the comfortable little pillow, which compressed to the size of her fist when uninflated. She dropped it into the front pocket with her Bible and MacDonald novel. All set. The pack rested, fat and easy, like a promise. Ana felt an unanticipated surge of excitement. Perhaps she was moving through her grief to a place where she could, finally, look beyond the next hours. This was the first time she felt anticipation for spending time—anywhere—since Frank died. Ana felt that if she gave it too much study it would scare her senseless. She turned away from the thought and deliberately picked up the heavy book on the table, carefully opening it to the postcard with the Mark Strand poem which she used as a bookmark. Idly, Ana wondered if she'd ever send that one to anybody. She settled back on the couch to read.

Chapter 10

When Ana walked up to the youth house—an old parsonage behind the church which had been converted for the use of the children and teenagers in the congregation—the church van was pulled up and the gear already loaded on top. Ana would have a seat to herself in the back.

When Ana went on the church trip to the Keys every summer, she could never believe the colors. So bright. She loved the colors but knew, like the speaker in Edna St. Vincent Millay's poem, they were not for everyday:

I know I am but summer to your heart (Sonnet XXVII)
Edna St. Vincent Millay, 1892 - 1950

 I know I am but summer to your heart,
And not the full four seasons of the year;

And you must welcome from another part
Such noble moods as are not mine, my dear.
No gracious weight of golden fruits to sell
Have I, nor any wise and wintry thing;
And I have loved you all too long and well
To carry still the high sweet breast of Spring.
Wherefore I say: O love, as summer goes,
I must be gone, steal forth with silent drums,
That you may hail anew the bird and rose
When I come back to you, as summer comes.
Else will you seek, at some not distant time,
Even your summer in another clime.

What was it about travel which made Ana whimsical? When she rode the train to visit Bellingham, or even the simple church van to the

Keys, something enlarged her. She reached, in travel, beyond the silly concerns of self and managed to forget them for a time; travel rested her in a way nothing else, not even reading, did. It took her back to standing on the shore as a small child, listening to her father speak about the universe and beyond. He taught her, young, how to navigate by the stars, seeming to assume she would not only be alright but more than; that she was vital and would contribute something necessary to the human race. In the end that is what he had done—contribute. He invented the Space Shuttle, came up with it; even after losing his friends to the tragedy of Apollo 1. He soldiered on. More, he fathered children he fully believed would contribute as much, more. Ana often found herself wondering, *what do I offer?*

Standing on the white, white sand of Islamorada, listening to the sweet chorus from the opened windows of the chapel, Ana knew it didn't matter; if she could only hold onto the fact of her presence in, her participation in, the human condition she would do what it was intended she do. Faith, that was the key. Her father had so much of that. As he lay dying, unable to speak, she'd leaned close and told him, *if I have as much integrity in me as you have in your little finger, I must be an amazing person.*

Ana laughed at herself. She dropped her towel and as she had done in childhood when she felt the need for anything—validation, emptiness, fullness, clarity—she plunged into the sea. As her father taught her so many Augusts ago, she floated. Ana allowed the sun to work its magic, the sea to support her in all its wise mystery. It would all be alright. It would. Nobody could ever take from Ana the foundation she was given by her parents, faith in a loving, benevolent God who waited for her to begin the greatest adventure of all. She felt the light on her skin, the salt drying on her face, and the living, breathing world underneath, gliding by. Ana dozed and relaxed into the salt sea supporting her, dreaming of the day when all would be known.

I wish I knew you sooner. I wish we hadn't got off to a bad start; I wish I knew you were beautiful then. What do you think? Do you think in Heaven, we will meet again. I'm sorry, what I did. What we do. Who knew when we were young how much it would matter? Do you know that song, the Verve Pipe, we were only freshmen, or something. I wish I'd said yes. I wish I'd let you be my friend. I might not have lost him, my brother. I might—I might have been better, little ugly girl, if I let you be my friend.

Ana woke. It was the first time she remembered falling asleep on the water. She was close to shore, the tide must be rising; it didn't scare her but it certainly surprised her. What had she been dreaming? Something involving sun, water, childhood. Oh, well. It was gone. And chapel was over; time to go to work. She generally had a visitor or two after chapel.

As she had thought down here before, Travis MaGee books were perfect reading for the Keys. There were a couple of them, and *Condominium* by the same author, on the bookshelf in her cabin, next to the dinette set like something out of 1952—all chrome and mottled red vinyl. Ana loved her long evenings in the cabin reading. The lamp next to the wicker couch was tall, and the old shade cast a melty yellow glow over the pages. Sometimes she fell asleep reading, something which never happened in Robinson, and woke with a slight chill on her skin from the salty air coming through the screens. Here, even though the cabin had air conditioning, at night she slept with it off and the windows as wide as the windows had been kept in her childhood. She could hear the sea, not the removed sound of pounding waves at Haven Beach through insulated windows, heavily draped; but close, gentle; shushing against the shore under the moonlight. Cicadas pitched their constant whine like white noise and even when she was relaxed—not tired at all—Ana drifted. She wondered if perhaps this relaxation, this security, had less to do with the rustic cabin and the sea and more to do with an identity—a role to play. Here, she was one of a small group and though they were light and benign, there were expectations. She would be here in the cabin each night from seven-thirty until ten, ready to listen.

This trip Ana had no campers come to her but Julia Morrow, the mother of two of the younger girls, dropped by every night. Ana had the feeling she needed to get away from the bunk-room; she didn't really seem to want to talk. They would drink a cup of tea together at the table, and Julia go over the plans she and the other chaperones had for the girls for the next day, written in a tablet of yellow notebook paper. It was understood Ana was always welcome on the outings. Sometimes she did join the campers and chaperones on the beach out front or walking into town for ice cream in the afternoons so as not to seem standoffish, but mostly Ana politely declined the day trips. Three days it rained heavily while the van was gone. Ana spent those in the cabin napping off and on, fixing small, elaborate meals for herself in the late afternoon. She'd picked up a few groceries—the church provided each of the chaperones and Ana an allowance for spending; Ana spent hers on postcards and food—and always had something good to eat waiting for Julia when she knocked on the kitchen door around eight.

Ana was pleased, in the way one is pleased to discover there are new adventures within the self even after decades of living, that she was able to cook again. This was the first time that happened since Frank died. As she did in the beginning of her marriage, she started with baked goods. Like learning to walk again, she make cookies and a six layer chocolate cake, and of course a key lime pie. When Julia left, Ana sent whatever was left from that afternoon's cooking with her, to take to the other moms in the bunkhouse. She didn't enjoy the eating so much as the process of cooking. She followed recipes she'd never seen before from a book on the shelf, one of those fundraiser cookbooks which often contain the best recipes, and a story with each:

Grandma Moxie's Best Buttermilk Biscuits

This comes from Grandma down to mother to me, and is much requested at family gatherings. Most people think this is a Southern recipe, but Grandma came from Quebec in 1891 with her father and seven brothers, after her mother died. She was six and already knew how to cook. She kept a biscuit bowl floured and ready and made a double batch every morning of her life, first for her father and brothers, then for my grandfather and the children, and finally for me and my sisters when we visited Johnson City every summer. I still have the biscuit bowl, and try to carry the tradition. The secret, she always said, was the cast iron skillet with lard heated for five minutes at 450 before dropping the biscuits in and turning them once with a fork. You know they will come out right if they pop up with that turn, just a bit.

Maisie Mae Benefield
Atlanta, Georgia
Druid Hills Baptist Church

2 cups flour
¼ t. salt
1 T. baking powder
2 T. lard
½ cup buttermilk, cold

Put 1 tablespoon lard in a cast iron skillet and put in oven. Heat oven to 450. Sift together first three ingredients into floured biscuit bowl. Cut in remaining lard, then mix with your hands, squeezing until lard is evenly distributed through flour mixture. Using wooden stirring spoon, slowly and gently stir in buttermilk, just until moist and hangs together in a ball of dough. Hand pat out on floured surface—cutting board, plate, or counter, whatever's handy. Flour top of dough as needed to keep from getting biscuits stuck in jar. Do not over-knead the dough, just pat it down once, turn it over once, and cut the biscuits out. After cutting, squeeze remaining dough into small uglies for little children or dogs. They both like these and it makes them feel special. Leave biscuits alone until oven is preheated or for five minutes, whichever is longer.

Take skillet out of oven carefully. This will be very hot. Small children and dogs should wait on the couch or floor by it at this point—you can reward them for listening with uglies. Set skillet on stove top, and one by one drop biscuits and uglies into hot lard, turning each with a fork as you do. Do this quickly and get them in the oven. Cook for five minutes then turn down, without opening door, to 350 for eleven minutes. Serve hot, cold, or anytime up to a week later. No need to refrigerate leftovers. Cover and store biscuit bowl at room temperature.

Small children and dogs. Wonderful. Ana made the biscuits. They were pretty good, but she had a feeling the floured, unwashed biscuit bowl handed down through the family was key. Along with the lard; the local market only had all-vegetable shortening. Ana made her own buttermilk. The date on the cookbook was 1984, a fundraiser for the Women's Missionary Union, Druid Hills Baptist Church. She wondered if Maisie Mae was here with a youth group, or if the WMU made a trip to the Keys. One of these days Ana was going to go through the bookshelf and look more closely at the books. There were perhaps a hundred, all five shelves were full. Someone must take care of the cabin when it was unoccupied; the books were in fairly good shape for being so close to the sea.

Wouldn't it be nice to have a journal, here, for everyone who stayed to put in a page? Like a guesthouse or a bed and breakfast. Ana stayed, with Frank, a couple of times at bed and breakfasts. To be fair, they tried two; one in Vermont and one in Chapel Hill. And hated both. The whole concept itched at Ana like a mosquito bite between the shoulder blades. She—and Frank too, it turned out—did not want to pay a lot of money to somebody to pretend to be a guest in their home. She didn't want to make small talk in a parlor in the evening, or chat politely with strangers or an innkeeper at breakfast. Ana liked to be anonymous on holiday. So did Frank. She hoped bed and breakfast establishments were a fad which would fade. Along with yoga, selfies, reality television, stand up paddleboarding, pilates, and facebook. But, especially, yoga on standup paddleboards. Ridiculous. The thought of fads made her think of Catherine Hilldale, her oldest, and now only, friend in New Jersey. Catherine and Ana watched earth shoes and pet rocks come and go. It was Catherine who introduced Ana to the town of Robinson; she owned a house in Haven Beach and rented it to Ana and Frank when they first moved north. Catherine spent part of November and December in Haven, from Thanksgiving until Christmas, doing an annual deep clean and needed repairs on her rental house. Ana hadn't seen her since Frank's funeral, but they talked on the phone sometimes. Ana sent her a card once in a while.

Ana chose a postcard with a drawing of two stylized sunbathers in fifties-era bikinis. She used a purple pen she found in a kitchen drawer.

Catherine,

I'm in the Keys with the church youth group at our annual camp. Beautiful here, not nearly as crowded on the beach as Haven gets this time of year. I thought of you and me at the Jersey shore when I saw this card. Off for a swim,

Ana

Chapter 11

Every morning at ten Ana went down to the beach. She kept her habit of sunscreening up before leaving the cabin, but was still getting some color since she spent the hotter hours at the beach. She missed her sun shelter; the easy-ups offered no privacy. But they did offer shade. The beach actually belonged to the camp, with public access, but few people who weren't in residence there bothered to walk all the way from the small parking lots at either end of the Baptist camp grounds. When the girls and chaperones were off on a day trip—once to the Miami Aquarium, another time to Key West, twice to the Everglades—Ana had the beach mostly to herself, so she had privacy anyway. There were a couple of Adirondack chairs under one shelter, stacks of folding beach chairs leaning against the poles of the other.

Ana was surprised how much she enjoyed the company of the campers and younger women on the days they all stayed in camp and went to the beach. She would sit in one of the sturdier chairs and watch the girls play in the water then run up every now and then to drain one of the bottles of water in ice from the coolers in a few gulps, or grab an orange or banana from the paper bag in the other chair next to Ana. These were Florida beach girls who didn't need to be warned or reminded about the sun or to hydrate. They were fluent swimmers, some were surfers, but there was no real surf here and they laughed and horsed around on sturdy canvas rafts or played Frisbee or smacked a beach ball back and forth in the water. They built elaborate sandcastles together above the high tide line, making it a challenge to work together each day, coming up with new designs. It might even be an assigned activity. Ana had no idea; but they laughed and argued and used children's beach buckets from the equipment locker in the shed next to the bunkhouse, and miniature rakes and shovels and molds for sand.

The day of the trip to Pennekamp everyone was in a good mood. It had been rainy the day before, but this was one of those rare, golden days at the end of summer; breezy, perfect. Ana made a huge batch of sugar cookies the day before. They took a cooler full of sandwiches, fruit, and water, and all the snorkeling gear, and set off in the church van at ten-thirty. It was a Friday; they were to travel back to Robinson the next day. School started on Tuesday. The girls were excited both to get home and to start school; they'd spent the rainy afternoon the day before shopping for gifts for their families and picking up souvenirs.

Pennekamp is the only U.S. underwater national park. Ana was comfortable on the boat going out to the reef, but some of the girls were nervous. Ana was a little disappointed they no longer had the catamaran rentals as an option; the snorkel boats were all captained by an employee and were power boats. There were small cats at the church camp. She had taken a few of the girls out and taught them some of the basics. Still, she intended to have a good time. The mate gave a brief lesson on snorkeling. Ana had her red library bag with her mask, snorkel and fins in it. She wore her new brown one piece, a long-sleeved white t-shirt, and a pair of nylon shorts she bought when she bought her flip-flops. Her gear was a set Frank bought for her twenty years ago on the Big Island of Hawaii. It had held up well and she knew from experience that the fins were just right; her feet wouldn't be sore tomorrow when she woke up. Some of the girls rented fins, and Ana talked them into bringing socks to wear under them.

The ten campers slipped into the water and immediately fanned out next to the boat, just over the reef. The moms and Ana stayed aboard for a while to watch the girls, make sure they were comfortable and didn't spread out too far. Ana drank a bottle of water and ate a turkey and cheese sandwich. She'd sit for a while and enjoy being out here.

When the girls first went off the dive platform, one by one, there was lots of laughter and calling back and forth, *come on, Maya, get wet! Don't put your mask on yet, Lu, get in first and get your hair wet! Somebody come over here, I think I see the statue!* As soon as they all got their masks on everything was suddenly quiet. The water lapped lazily against the hull, the captain smoked a cigarette, and the mate reached into the cooler in the stern for a bottle of water.

"Julia," Ana asked, "Do you want to go in?"

"I think I'll stay up here for a while. Enjoy the peace and quiet. Are you going?"

"Sure." Ana dug her gear out of her bag, stashed her water bottle and sandwich baggie in it. "I'm going to head out from the stern, a little away from the girls."

Ana sat down on the diving platform, and put on her black and orange swim fins, then slipped into the water. It was cooler out here than close to shore, but still much warmer than the water in Haven Beach. Tropical, clear. Ana could see the bottom twenty feet below. She slipped under, then kicked up and grabbed her mask, with the snorkel attached, off the transom. She spit in it a couple of times, rubbed the spit around with her fingers, then rinsed the mask and put it on. There were more PC ways to prep a mask, expensive concoctions in little bottles at the shops, but Ana was comfortable with the old-fashioned method. She drifted off.

The variety of life on the reef always startled Ana; the colors of the sea fans and anemone and coral, reds and yellows and oranges, brown and purple and pink—with the sunlight winking down through clear green water—hypnotized her. The girls had been cautioned against touching the living reef. Eels hid there, and spiny lobsters, even an occasional beautiful, deadly lion-fish. Ana liked to hang, still, in the water and see what swam by below her. She could see her shadow, arms spread, feet elongated by the fins, against the coral below. The sun was directly overhead. It was a strange sensation when she saw the shark emerge from her own shadow as if it were coming out of a body into the light.

A thresher about four feet long, sinuous tail curving like a scythe, propelling the animal lazily along in the direction of open water beyond the reef. It was swimming away from the boat, away from the snorkelers. Ana felt her heart quicken, but stayed still. The shark knew she was there but didn't turn. Instead, it glided away into the distance.

It was unusual to see a shark out here. They tended to stay away from the boats and the disruption of people in the water. Ana was nipped once as a child in Flagler Beach, got a couple of stitches and a lot of attention at school. She wasn't really scared of sharks, but she was careful. Ana never wore jewelry in the water. She didn't thrash about. The shark was out of sight. Ana propelled herself over to where the girls were and looked down. Lots of angelfish and a couple of sea turtles; no more sharks.

By the time they arrived back at camp at 2:30, Ana was beat. She went to her cabin for a quick shower and a nap. She woke up at six disoriented from sleeping in the afternoon and made herself a cup of coffee. Ana had planned well regarding using up the food she'd purchased; she was leaving a few staples. And, *The Goldfinch*. Ana knew that forever after this, she would smell and feel and see in her mind's eye this place when she thought of the book. She took one of her postcards and wrote, *contributed by Ana Mills of Robinson, Florida, to the little library in this cabin. There's extra postcards: please use them as bookmarks and leave your name and recommendation on a book. I loved this book: it took me places I will never go. The language is baroque and lovely. September 3rd, 2015.* On the front of the postcard was a recipe for Key Lime pie and a photograph of a giant slice.

After her coffee Ana walked down to the beach. She was surprised to see some of the campers in the water, then remembered chapel for this evening would be moved to tomorrow morning right before they left for Robinson. Lita Marquez, a small, athletic girl whose parents owned one of the condominium complexes on the north end of Robinson, ran up to Ana. "Miss Ana, take me sailing!" Lita was never able to sit, or stand, still. She was a bundle of energy hopping from foot to foot waiting on Ana's answer, even though the sand was shadowed and cool at this time of day.

"It's a little late, Lita."

"Oh please! We haven't been out this time of day before, we're always in chapel! The breeze is just about right, isn't it, like you taught me! My mom will come!"

Without waiting for further comment from Ana, Lita raced off to the bunkhouse. It would be nice to sail for a bit this time of the evening; the colors of sun on the sea were so changeable now, winking mildly from the light cast between the trees, brighter further out where full sun still hit the rippling sea. The breeze was about seven knots. Not brisk, but sailable. Lita, Ana had seen, had taken advantage of using the catamarans quite a bit since Ana worked with her on the basics the first few days of camp. She was a bright girl, quick and polite, not a bit spoiled by her privileged childhood that Ana could tell.

Lita and her mother, Jane, were coming through the trees.

"Okay, Lita, I'll go out with you. I don't have a lot left to show you, you've got the basics, except for remembering what to tell your crew, but that will come. Get some of the other girls to help you get the cat in the water, and your mom and I will join you."

"Ana, isn't it a little late to be going out on the boat?" Jane asked as she and Ana stepped from opposite pontoons onto the bow end of the tramp.

"No, it'll be okay. We'll just go down wind for a bit, then tack back. Here, sit next to me," Ana said, "Lita will head us out on a reach, that way." Ana pointed to the northeast. Jane sat next to her on the starboard side of the tramp as Lita hopped agilely up from the pontoon onto the stern. The tramp was a canvas deck, laced to the pontoons. Lita guided the boat out past the small waves, left hand on the rudder, right pulling the sheet in and locking the line into a cleat with practiced ease.

"Don't drop the line, Lita, " Ana suggested. "Keep it in your hand at all times."

Lita did as she was told, smiled, and shook her black hair back over her shoulders without letting go of either rudder or line. She was a natural. Ana looked over the side, noticing through the clear water a pair of dark shadows following them just off the starboard, twenty feet astern. They were a good hundred yards out, now, and she kept an eye on the shadows. Lita looked at Ana—as she'd been taught, keeping an eye on everything including her passengers, and her eyes widened when she saw what Ana was watching. Then, everything happened at once.

"Sharks!" Lita yelled, jerking the line toward herself, out of the cleat, swinging the boom and with it the bow around with a jerk to head back toward shore. Ana instinctively threw up her left arm to protect her head but even with it cushioning the blow felt a painful knock as her own elbow connected with her forehead. Unable to stop herself she knocked into Jane, who managed to hang onto the tramp, and went backwards into the water.

As Ana flipped around beneath the water, she noticed that her left arm wasn't doing what it was supposed to. She pushed herself to the surface using her right and kicking her feet. Fifty feet away, Lita was fighting with the boat to get it turned around again; Jane lay on the front of the tramp, looking worriedly back at Ana.

"Lita," Ana called, "Don't worry! It isn't—" Just then she felt water push up beneath her feet. Something big, and strong and warm, rose up between them. A fin came up right in front of her and her right arm instinctively went down to it. As soon as her fingers closed over the fin, Ana felt the animal give a powerful flip to its tail. She shot forward toward the boat at incredible speed, left arm hanging uselessly down. The dolphin stopped right next to the port pontoon, then as quickly as it rose dropped from between her legs and disappeared. Ana's heart thumped in her chest. Her left forearm began to throb. Jane reached down to grab it.

"No," Ana said, "You're going to have to help me get up there without grabbing that arm. I think it's broken."

"But, Ana, we have to hurry! The sharks!" Lita shrieked.

"Calm down, Lita, and think. They weren't sharks. That was a pair of dolphins. One of them brought me over to the boat. It was amazing. I wonder why. I wasn't in any trouble, really."

"Well," Jane said, carefully tugging Ana onto the tramp backwards, "not that you know of. Besides, maybe it sensed you're hurt."

And she was. Once she was out of the water, her left arm throbbed. There was no visible wound, but it felt cracked. Ana stripped her t-shirt off her other arm, leaving the neck on, and she and Jane immobilized her left arm as best they could with that. Lita, calmer, slowly tacked her way to the beach and ran the cat up onto it. They helped Ana to her cabin. She put on one of her warm up suits over her bathing suit. Jane, who was the official leader of the group, took Ana to the hospital for an x-ray, assuring her this was covered under the church's policy and she wouldn't have to use her own insurance.

With the help of pain medicine Ana slept in the next morning. She slept right through chapel, and with a bread bag over her cast managed a shower. The break was a crack in the ulna; the cast wrapped around the base of her thumb and ended above her elbow. Ana had a sling to put it in once she was dressed. Unfortunately she was left-handed; writing was going to be a challenge. Still, it could have been worse. School was over for the semester. Although her wrist and elbow were immobilized, she could still use her fingers. Once the cast was on the pain was nearly nonexistent; even before, it didn't hurt very much. Lita felt terrible, but Ana reassured her and told her she had done a fine job getting them all back to the beach quickly. All the way back to Robinson the girls talked about how easy it was to mistake a dolphin for a shark in certain light. They laughed and were in high spirits—everyone was glad Ana was going to be all right and that school would be starting the next week.

Ana was given the entire back seat of the van to herself. Perhaps because of the pain medicine and the movement of the vehicle, she drifted. Not sleeping, not dreaming really, but her defenses against thinking must have been low. Her mind wandered to strange places. Where she was at this moment seemed unreal, seemed far from her: four years ago she had known none of these people. She didn't know them now.

If anyone from her old life saw her now they wouldn't know Ana. Not Frank, not Catherine: nobody. Her own children didn't count, or her grandchildren; your progeny never did know you. What she chose in order to survive after losing Frank and everything which went with her life with him seemed unreal. Could a person actually walk out of one life and into another? Redesign the self step-by-step, moment-by-moment, until all that was recognizable from the past disappeared around the curve of a one-way street? Everyone knew, cognitively, that you could not repeat the past, but could you erase it? Erase your connection to that self. And had that self been a choice, too? It never seemed so before. Ana's life before seemed destined and acceptable and orderly. Yet now was when *she* was orderly. Cool and collected, even getting hurt on the water, even falling in the deep.

What had she done? Obviously she could not retrieve her old life—even if now she could face being a widow in her old house, her old neighborhood. Her things were all gone and she could not imagine dragging around the extra weight, messing with long hair, a closet full of shoes and clothes and winter things; cooking huge meals, even if she could find somebody to eat them. She liked being alone, being mostly invisible; she liked being quiet. Ana found that being a volunteer everywhere she was meant being the low person on the totem pole. The higher up the pole, the more people had to say. Volunteers could pick up a list or task and disappear into the scenery. Why was she disappearing? Why did she need that?

Ana wondered if all roads led to where she was. Would Robin end up here one day? Ella? At the place where life was merely solitude, waiting? Observing without ever really reaching out, without holding onto anyone or anything. Breaking her arm, even, had happened at a remove— the dolphin a remarkable thing but like watching it happen to somebody else. That, yes, the event, the remarkable thing happened to her, but with the personality she had stepped into nobody in the group even really asked her to tell it. They asked Lita, they asked Jane, and it became a story, but they didn't ask Ana. Because she had always had this wall around her, this cocoon of privacy and peace, this separateness, it seemed natural not to disturb her as she drifted in and out. When they drove through a hard rain north of Miami and all the traffic slowed, and nobody talked because what was the point with the noise of the storm? and Ana closed her eyes and drifted, she might as well be the only person on earth, hunkered back in a cave.

Those were some powerful pain pills. Rather than seeming to do anything for her arm, they seemed to have a paradoxical effect on Ana's brain—she was thinking too much about things which it would do her no good to delve into. This was the life she had. It was a deliberate choice. Did it matter if the people of Robinson had no idea who she was, or who she had been before? She served them well. She contributed. Did it matter that her purpose was singular, selfish, the drowning of grief and despair with light work, too easy? Did it matter that all she felt, even breaking a bone, was numb, that she didn't really care for any of these people? Her motives in volunteering were selfish, even nefarious. But the work got done and she certainly wasn't ready for a real, regular job. She hadn't worked since just after high school, eons ago, and she had no skills to speak of. If she finished her degree she'd probably find something in the field of social work much like she did now; volunteer coordinator for some public facility or a nonprofit. Running some local public awareness effort or group. She couldn't imagine taking an actual job as a social worker; all that intimacy. All that singularity, specificity. Human experience in the ear, on the page. Collaborating in the interest of changing lives for the better. What was for the better? If all roads lead to grief wasn't working on *better* just a big, misleading lie?

When Ana got back to Robinson she felt like she could sleep for a week. All the drifting in and out in the van left her headachy and irritable. She was thirsty. As soon as she got to the church she went into the bathroom at the youth house and flushed the pain pills down the toilet, reserving only three in case it was a mistake. She'd know soon enough if she was actually hurting, but she'd put up with an awful lot of hurt not to go through the odd stasis she'd experienced on the trip back. She knew the feeling would pass soon; the camp had been restful for the most part, so Ana decided to get right back into her routine and work her regular shift at the hospital. Ironing the uniforms might be a bit of a challenge for a while; but at least this weekend she could wash, dry, and hang any smocks which had been left for her in the locker room.

By the time her cast came off Ana was busy getting ready for her trip to Bellingham. The weather turned cool in early October. While she still worked out some mornings at the University, she had decided against going on to graduate school when she finished her degree. Spending cold and rainy days researching interesting jobs she found quite a few for people with a B.A. in social work. Developing a resume was difficult. Ana had very little experience working for or with people so she began to cultivate a few relationships. She decided it was alright to leave her age and marital status off the resume. After all, prospective employers couldn't ask by law the answer to either question.

Most of the jobs Ana saw—and right now she was only getting a taste for what the market was—were in other towns and she would have to move. Ana could only hope something came up in or near Robinson. She decided she was unwilling to leave Florida. She'd been raised here, she intended to die here. Although the weather was sometimes mercilessly hot and wet she loved living near the ocean. Anywhere you were in the state you were never more than eighty miles from the ocean or the Gulf. Ana liked that. She was planning beyond the next month for the first time in a very long time.

For references, Ana had been thinking about who would look best. She could give Catherine as a personal reference. She'd even actually worked for her off and on over the years in her cleaning business when she needed money. Catherine called Ana when she was in a pinch and Ana went out to the rental house and cleaned there. When the children were in elementary school she'd worked a bit as a laundress for Catherine's upstart maid service, gathering up the loads of linens in the mornings, spending her days watching the clothes go around at the local Laundromat then taking them back around to the houses Catherine and her two employees were working on, finishing before the children got out of school. She'd done this for four years three days a week, for pocket money. It hadn't been what Ana thought of as a real job but Catherine now had businesses in several cities, and had made a name for herself—she was a good reference to have. Together, when the time came, they would come up with some title for the work Ana had done which would serve her purpose.

Dr. Brewster wrote Ana a letter of reference at her request. She let him believe it was for applications to graduate school—she'd asked for it over e-mail before deciding against continuing her education beyond undergrad. But she thought it would serve; it was good to have one of her professors willing to recommend her.

The final relationship Ana cultivated with an eye to the future was with Tiffany Anderson. They were now eating lunch together one day a week at the hospital cafeteria, and Ana trained her as a volunteer at the hospital. After seeing Ana's cast in September when Ana worked her next shift at the library, Tiffany asked if there was anything she could do for Ana which would help. Ana surprised herself by mentioning the ironing at the hospital.

"Ana!" Tiffany laughed, "You're a wonder. I'll tell you what; I want to start working at the hospital, too, and I will be happy to come in and iron for you if you'll keep me company while I do. What day do you normally do the ironing?"

"I start Saturday mornings around eleven."

"Saturday! Well, I guess I could do that. Edgar usually has some city thing to attend to on Saturdays and I'm often expected to go, and I never enjoy myself. If I'm working at the hospital I'm sure that will be acceptable.

I'll tell you what—I'll meet you at eleven, work for an hour, then we can have lunch and finish up. Will that work?"

So every Saturday Ana now spent with Tiffany. While she missed the solitude and resented the intrusion on the separateness she'd carefully built, Tiffany had a surprisingly good attitude about doing the ironing. Ana put the uniforms in the washer before starting her shift on Friday night, put them in the dryer midway through, then took a break and hung them, still damp, to let some of the wrinkles fall out. The smocks were the only thing which needed starch and ironing; the uniform pants were the responsibility of individual volunteers. If there were too many smocks for one load, Ana started another at ten before Tiffany arrived to iron.

By the time Ana's cast came off, Tiffany was used to the task of preparing the uniforms. She told Ana she wanted to continue. This happened on a dreary October Saturday afternoon in the hospital cafeteria. Tiffany worked Saturdays, and did a turn on the front desk on Monday afternoons as well, so just like Ana she had two meal vouchers a week for the cafeteria. It made sense to eat together Saturdays. Sometimes they had dinner on Monday nights after Tiffany's volunteer hours since Ana took fall semester off to travel.

"Ana," Tiffany said as she stirred her ranch dressing though her chef salad with her fork, "Why don't you let me keep the ironing job for now, since you'll be gone in November and December? Anytime I can't get it done I'll put a note on the white board, and people won't complain anyway; they're used to having to do it themselves when you're out of town, right?"

Ana finished spreading mayonnaise on her hamburger bun, then carefully placed her lettuce and tomato back on it. She didn't like to order her burger with mayo on it, she preferred to do it herself to keep the lettuce from getting wilted and soggy. She took a contemplative bite of her cheeseburger and nodded to Tiffany, okay.

After six weeks of spending hours each week together, Tiffany understood the job of keeping a conversation going with Ana fell largely on her. She didn't mind.

The more time Ana spend with Tiffany the less she was reminded of Midgie. Tiffany was kind—she'd learned this from the way she stepped right in to help Ana after she broke her arm. She also had a complicated marriage, and wasn't very interested in money. And, like Ana, she was a Christian, not a Whateverian like Midgie. Ana was secretly pleased Tiffany hated fads, too, but she was more vocal about it, laughing so hard at the close encounter the local paddleboard yoga club had with a bull shark in the river she'd had to turn off the iron, sit down while she as trying to tell Ana about, then simply hand Ana the newspaper from the table to read about it. " Moron....born.. every minute!" Tiffany roared, clutching her side, guffawing, tears seeping from her squenched eyes. Very unMidgielike.

Now, Ana said, "Sure. Do you want to give me a ride to the train station next Monday? I could take the bus. I usually do."

"Oh sure. We can stop at the courthouse in DeLand and look at the paintings there, if you want. Have you seen them? No? Magnificent! There's a Jackson Stuart of the shootout with Ma and Pa Barker I particularly love."

As usual Ana had very little luggage for her trip. She would be on the train five days, four nights; she was careful to bring a couple of good books to get her started—she could always pick one up somewhere along the way if she ran out of reading material. She took two of her favorites: *To Kill a Mockingbird* and *Alas, Babylon* and one she hadn't read before, David Brin's *The Postman*. Ana love post-apocalyptic books. Her great Aunt Sadie had grown up with Harper Lee. She remembered Sadie visiting when Ana was a small child. Sadie told her about Boo Radley and the children in the neighborhood, and what Sadie called "that little sissy boy" Dill from the book who grew up to become Truman Capote.

Sadie came to visit when Ana was a little girl. She seemed old then, but must've been in her early sixties. She married Ana's father's uncle Roscoe, who helped raise him after his parents died in Mississippi. Ana loved it when her father's relatives came. Sadie was different from the others. She traveled alone, a widow by then. She seemed in good shape and in those days it was unusual for a woman to travel alone. Ana's father liked to tell how when he was a young man in Europe his first summer away from Georgia Tech the Navy sent him across the Atlantic for his first training cruise. He and some mates got liberty for four days in France. They took the train from Cherbourg to Paris. It was 1952. He and his friends ran into Sadie traveling by herself, at the Eifel Tower; she took them all to dinner.

As Ana waited in the station for her train—which as usual was late—after Tiffany dropped her off, she thought of Sadie. As a child she'd started to feel sorry for Sadie, a widow alone in the world; no children, no husband. But Sadie seemed so happy, so contained with her one suitcase and smart clothes, always a hat, gloves, and matching bag, that Ana couldn't. Sadie didn't fit into any of the "relatives" categories in Ana's young mind: slews of cousins and big noisy families on her mother's side in Atlanta. Big houses in the country in Mississippi, everybody looking like her father.

Sadie was full of stories. She was afraid of nothing and certainly not lonely. She had a cousin who led the raid on Tokyo at the beginning of World War II—a sense of adventure, Sadie said, ran in her family. She'd stayed a few weeks in Flagler then taken the train to the Keys to see where Hemingway lived. Ana realized that when she met her, Sadie was only a few years older than Ana was now. Ana was going to a place where she could feel at home, to her son's house; Sadie had no children. Suddenly Ana felt glad for the child she had been, and that she recognized there was no reason to pity her father's widowed aunt, that Sadie was happy, enjoying her travels. While Ana didn't feel a sense of adventure, she felt something. She had it: relief. She was relieved to get out of Robinson, to have a few days to make the transition to Bellingham by herself. At Robin's she'd have a room and bath with a kitchen alcove over the garage, which suited her fine.

Ana settled into her accommodations in the sleeper car quickly. The steward brought her coffee and a piece of blueberry pie, warm, with fresh whipped cream. There was a white rose in a crystal vase on the tray, and the steward took her dinner order. She would have it in her room. Ana always gained a little weight when she traveled because she wasn't walking and swimming every day. The meals were larger than her usual fare; she also had two complementary snacks every day. But, she allowed herself that. She would be hiking with the boys all over Bellingham, rain or shine. It was one of their favorite things to do and they enjoyed sharing their town, and the mountains and sea surrounding it, with Ana.

There was a new addition to the room since she'd last traveled by train; a small television faired into the wall across from the comfortable armchair. Ana had her own toilet, shower, and sink, complete with toiletries. She left the television off and watched the scenery as the train got underway, facing forward Ana could see the engine when the train took curves; she was six cars back.

For some reason Ana slept better on the train that she ever did in Robinson. She dozed off and on during the day, went to bed early at night, and slept the night through despite frequent stops. The sleeping cars were much quieter than the regular cars, with passengers embarking and disembarking with much less frequency. Ana found a use for the television even though she watched very little her five days aboard; there were music channels. She found it pleasant to leave classical music playing while she read and while she slept. A couple of nights she ate her evening meals in the dining car. For that she dressed up; once in her paisley dress with a black sweater, once in her all-purpose black dress with a beautiful pale blue silk scarf over her shoulders. Mornings she stayed in her pajamas and ate breakfast in bed. When she was ready for lunch, after her shower and watching the changing landscape for a while, Ana went to the dining car to eat and her steward put her room in order, changed the linens and towels and restocked her supply of toiletries and bottled water.

Ana didn't run out of reading material. She left the train at a couple of stations to pick up postcards; she bought some in Washington D.C. and in Chicago, and at a few of the smaller cities in the Midwest. She wrote to each of her grandchildren and to Catherine; she wrote to Tiffany. She took long naps, waking to watch the sunset each afternoon.

Robin and Marie met the train in Seattle. It was an hour and a half to Bellingham. Ana didn't mind at all that, as usual, it was raining. She arrived in the afternoon and had eaten on the train, so they drove straight home. Robin brought her a light wool coat; in the pocket was the inevitable umbrella. "In Florida," Ana said as she hugged Robin, "We just get wet!"

Robin laughed. "I remember, Mom, but you'd get sick, here."

Robin looked more like Frank the older he got. Wide brown eyes, curly-lashed, wrinkling at the outside corners nowadays more deeply than before. His chestnut curls were shot with gray and thinning at the temples. Like his father was, he was a hair under six feet tall with powerful shoulders, square hands.

"Ana, I love your short hair! So elegant," Marie ran her hand over the top of Ana's head as she hugged her. Nearly as tall as her husband, Marie was willowy and blond with pale Nordic skin. She was deceptively frail-looking, but Ana had seen her hike ten miles looking as cool as she did right now. With almost anybody else the gesture would have bothered Ana, but she loved Marie dearly and there was not a pretentious or insincere bone in her body.

"Get me to those grandsons!" Ana laughed. It always took a bit of time on the west coast before Ana adjusted to the ocean being on what felt like the wrong side. Heading north from Seattle to Bellingham, if felt like going south, but the sun was setting by the time they arrived at the house.

Chapter 12

Robin and Marie and their boys Lucas and Sam lived in a roomy arts and crafts bungalow on a wide, tree lined street close to the center of town. The garage was separate with a small apartment over it, with covered stairs on the outside. The apartment was where Ana stayed. Luke and Sam ran across the front porch and down the steps, Sam jumping the last few onto the walkway, and raced to the car to hug their grandmother. "Let me get out of the car," Ana laughed.

They both seemed to have grown inches just since Ana had seen them in Florida in July. "Grandma," said Luke, "we're going to take you on the new rails to trails paths this visit!"

"And don't forget, next week we're off two extra days from school and we're taking you camping on Whidbey Island," said Sam. Sam was tall and blond like his mother; taller, Ana noticed, even than Robin. Luke was stockier, with his father's curls but his mother's coloring.

"How about you two tote my bag up to my room. I'm going to say hello to the dogs."

The golden retrievers waited on either side of the front door like a matched set of canine sculptures. Ana was always surprised they remembered her, or seemed to, but as soon as she climbed the front steps, both tails thumped the wooden porch floor in unison. It was good to be in Bellingham.

The next day Ana and Marie went to the co-op to buy whatever Ana wanted to cook while Marie and Robin were on their trip. And she *did,* she was surprised to find, want to cook. They bought salmon and mixed wild rices Ana would cook with walnuts, pecans, spinach, mushrooms, carrots, and cumin. They bought apples and frozen blackberries for pies and cobblers, and chicken and carrots and onion and potatoes for chicken pot pie.

"We're all stocked on camping food," Marie said. "The boys are excited about taking you to Whidbey. They want to fish. You won't really be camping; there's a cabin. With a wood stove which works just like ours, a bunk-room for the boys, a bedroom for you. We're leaving you three the truck and taking the car to Seattle; we'll leave it in the employee lot at the station. I can't tell you how much we appreciate this." Marie's fair skin colored becomingly, "It'll be like a second honeymoon. We're doing the Grand Canyon trip! I've always wanted to see the Grand Canyon. And I'll tell you the truth, I'm kind of glad we're taking the train and not planning any camping or hiking. This will be—I don't know—luxurious! No meals to prepare, no trash to pack out or water and food to pack in. Heat! Air conditioning!"

Ana laughed. "I know what you mean. I loved my trip out. I slept, ate, read, and looked out the window, and that was about it. Wonderful. We'd better get back, you and Robin need to get on the road by one to make your train."

For the next couple of days Ana wandered the house and cooked slow, all-day meals; stews and pies and breads, and walked the dogs while her grandsons were in class. The house had double-paned windows and central heat, but this time of year Ana liked to keep a small fire going in the wood stove in the living room during the day. There was a deep, sea-foam green cloth couch and two old-fashioned goose-necked rocking chairs covered in blue floral tapestry. The bookshelves built into the wall across from the windows onto the front porch were filled not just with books, but with treasures gathered over the years on family outings; smooth stones from the shore, bits of driftwood and seashells, tiny pots filled with loamy soil and delicate ferns; dried leaves and vases filled with dried flowers. There were scatter rugs Marie fashioned from yarn and old clothes on the wooden floors. All through the house, even with the doors and windows shut, Ana could hear the music of beach-glass and driftwood chimes from the front porch. Just outside the kitchen, with a small picket fence around it to keep the dogs out, was an old-fashioned kitchen garden. Robin worked it with Luke's help. There were two apple trees in the corner of the yard opposite the garage against the back fence.

Each evening the boys ate until they were groaning then rinsed and stacked the dishes into the dishwasher before plopping down on the couch to watch television. Ana was still on east coast time, so eight o'clock felt like eleven to her and she turned in right after supper. She could barely keep her eyes open long enough to brush her teeth, change into the flannel pajamas she kept in the maple dresser next to the twin bed, and read a few pages. Even though her body clock was off for now it would serve her well for staying at the cabin. The boys would wake early to fish and she and the dogs wander through the woods and down to the shore to watch.

Luke and Sam packed the truck. Luke drove. The dogs had made this trip many times before. They sat in the backseat of the king cab Dodge with Sam. The ferry to Whidbey only took a half an hour; they caught the last one Friday evening. Ana sat inside on the upper deck and drank weak coffee in a paper cup with a poker hand. She laughed to herself as she got to the bottom; a busted flush, just like a Travis McGee novel.

Even though it was dark there was a full moon shining on the water, and the spikes of the firs and ridges on the San Juans poked black against the starry blue. Moonlight silvered the icy Pacific water. Ana never swam out here, and of course the boys wouldn't in November; but even in Monterey in summertime the water had been too cold for Ana. She always thought of this a business ocean, the Atlantic as play. The Pacific was all business; a serious prospect, and by comparison the warm and gentle Atlantic, with its rock-free, white sand beaches, seemed like a playground. Sure, she had seen it raging and angry, and she knew to be careful in the water and even on the beach. But the power of the Pacific, even crossing from the mainland in the ferry, was daunting and a little frightening to Ana. Although the water was calm it seemed alive, deep and powerful; a mysterious animal with little regard for human life.

Frank laughed and teased Ana when they were young and lived in California about her superstitious fear of the ocean. She'd been such a water girl in Florida. He'd surf, and Ana would keep a fire going on the beach for him to warm up by. Although she did little on vacation but read, cook, sleep—or perhaps because of that—she thought more of Frank than she did at home. It was as if relaxing (even her short hikes with the boys were relaxing) made her miss him. Keeping busy, staying tired, she didn't have as much time to think about him. When she'd take off her boots and wool socks, soak in a hot bath, she'd remember Frank's strong hands rubbing her feet at the end of the day while they watched Jeopardy! and Wheel of Fortune. She always told him, *I didn't know my feet hurt until you started doing that.* Frank would smile, slowly wag his fingers at her, and say, *That's just my left hand, honey. Wait 'til you see what I can do with my right.*

Ana wondered, when the boys spent their mornings fishing, kindly taking the dogs out first and locking them back in the cabin and starting a roaring fire in the stove, if this was what getting old was; lazing around in your pajamas until noon, reading, napping, going to bed early. Briefly, it crossed her mind that she might be ill, but Ana knew herself well enough to know better than that. It didn't occur to her that she kept very busy, perhaps too busy, in Florida until she got away. Also it was easier to slip into the relaxed mother and grandmother roles she was used to and shed her efficient new persona out here. The train trip gave her ample time to do that, to switch roles. Everybody, Ana supposed, showed different faces to different people. And everybody had secrets.

At the end of the week Ana and her grandsons tidied the cabin and drove back to Bellingham. A strong, windy rain kept them inside on the ferry ride. Marie and Robin had returned the day before. That night Marie cooked; when they got home the house smelled of a rich tomato sauce with pork sausage she'd made from tomatoes put up the previous summer; they had spaghetti with garlic toast, a Caesar salad and chianti. Ana was leaving the next day.

The boys disappeared into their rooms. Ana, Marie, and Robin carried wine into the living room. Rain pounded on the tin roof. Robin left the door of the Franklin stove open so they could watch the fire. It glinted off the copper flashing protecting the wall behind it and the slate protecting the floor. Beeswax tapers burned low on the English oak pub table in the dining room, and lightning glinted now and again, flashing green against the beach glass chimes that writhed and twisted in the wind below the porch roof.

"Mom," Robin said, his feet in heavy ragg socks resting easily in Marie's lap, "we'd love it if you'd think about coming out here to live with us. We don't need to rent out the apartment anymore, anyway it was too much trouble with students always moving on. I know you don't want to sell the beach house. But if you did, you could live here and still see Sis as much as ever. We could just all rent a house in Haven in July, and you wouldn't have to take care of that place by yourself."

Ana's mind was whirling. She carefully placed her wine glass on the coffee table. She frowned.

"Don't try to decide right now!" Marie said. " It's an open invitation. We'd love to have you here anytime. We hope you know that. We just haven't come right out and said it before. Keep it in mind."

Ana imagined what it would be like seeing family every day. She wondered if she'd slip right back into her old personality: gain weight, let her hair grow, buy too many clothes, frump through her days. Or she could come out here and stay who she had become: quiet, private, efficient. She wondered, fleetingly, what that would do to Robin—to see his mother in the role of busy volunteer, college student. Student! Now would be a great time to tell them she couldn't move for a year, she had to finish college. But did she? Why did she have to finish? And if she wanted to, couldn't she transfer? Besides, this was Robin and Marie's moment. She didn't want to steal their thunder.

"That is so sweet," Ana finally managed, "and to tell you the truth I am very glad you brought it up because it had honestly never occurred to me! I not only didn't realize you might want that someday, much less now! I have never thought of it! And I promise I will. I will give it some serious thought. I am really touched, you two. It isn't every couple who'd want an old lady living over the garage. Let's talk about it again when you come out in July. I'll try to have some sort of answer by then. I am not particularly attached to the house." She saw Robin's quick frown. "Oh, I know it means a lot to you and your sister, Robin; we all have a lot of memories at the beach house. But time does move on. I have to admit it just doesn't even feel like the same town that it did when we all stayed there as a family, with your Dad coming down too. It's not that it's particularly lonely, it's just different. I don't know that many people. And you all are so far away. Let's face it, I'm not getting any younger. I am touched, truly, and I'll think about it."

Marie raised her glass, smiled, and said, "To the future."

Chapter 13

The next day Ana rode with Robin to Seattle and caught the train. All the way back to Florida, as she watched America slide past her window, Ana thought about living in Bellingham. It would mean not taking this luxurious trip every year. Oh, well. Who knew what the future would bring? She might as well enjoy the now.

"Ana," Tiffany said as they climbed into her Lexus at the DeLand station, "you look positively wonderful! Your skin! So clear. And your hair's growing out. I never realized it was so curly! Doesn't Florida just feel like a wet blanket of humidity after the west coast? Of course it's wet in Washington, too, but a different kind of wet, you know? Not all hot and hard to breathe. Well, tell me about your trip."

"Positively decadent. I'll bet I gained ten pounds. I love the food on the train. And Robin and Marie, well, they offered to let me move into the apartment I use full time. They'd like me to. No pressure, they just want me to think about it."

"And give up your life here? All your friends? Oh, Ana, that would be terrible! Please don't do anything hasty, you're such a part of our town!" Ana saw Tiffany's eyes actually fill with tears. "Besides, I have a surprise for you. I'll give it to you tomorrow, okay?" She sniffled, wiped her nose with the side of her forefinger. "At lunch."

"Tiffany, I didn't say yes. I just told them I'd think about it. I wouldn't go for, oh, at least a year! Hey, take me straight to the hospital, will you? I'm on duty tonight. Here, look what I brought you." Ana dug around in her backpack and brought out a book on Lummi Indians and a Nootka carving of a salmon.

The next morning Ana woke up groggily as Tiffany's key turned in the door to the locker room at the hospital. She'd fallen asleep on the hospital bed in the corner after putting the smocks in the dryer. "I have the worst time adjusting to the time changes. I was actually an early riser in

Washington, but it'll take me a couple of weeks to get straightened around." She rubbed her eyes, and dug her toiletry kit out of her backpack, went in the bathroom to brush her teeth. She was starving; she hadn't eaten breakfast and it was already 11:30.

When Ana came out of the bathroom Tiffany was hanging the pink smocks on wire hangers, then hooking them over the top of the lockers. "Let's go eat. I'll iron these when we get back. You let them dry completely, today; we're going to need a lot of starch. They're pretty wrinkly." It was apparent from the spring in her step that Tiffany was back to her usual sunny self.

Ana got a bigger meal than usual. She'd put on weight in Washington. Her days and nights were screwed up, she could tell; she'd better watch it. She'd better get into the routine of eating breakfast if she didn't want to get big as a house. She'd go to the gym this afternoon; time to shake off the laziness of vacation and get back to it.

"Let's sit over here in the corner," Tiffany said. "I have something to give you. As a matter of fact, I hope it'll help a little with your decision about staying here instead of moving." That was just like Tiffany; to cleverly phrase something with exactly the slant she wanted you to take from it. Ana carried her tray and followed Tiffany to a booth tucked behind some vending machines with sandwiches, soups, little cups of cereal, and microwaveable pasta dishes.

Tiffany finished tossing her chef salad with ranch dressing and started impatiently drumming her fork on her orange plastic cafeteria tray, waiting for Ana to spread mayonnaise on her cheeseburger bun and squeeze a couple of packets onto her plate to dip her French fries in.

"Well, what is it Tiffany?" Ana finally said as she looked up from saying a silent grace.

Tiffany positively bounced in her seat, grinning from ear to ear; she dramatically reached slowly into her blue leather Coach hobo bag, looking straight at Ana the whole time, and smartly smacked the base of a small Lucite trophy, diamond shaped with one point resting in a square gray marble base, on the table between their trays.

Ana Mills
St. Vincent Memorial Hospitals
Volunteer of the Year
2015

Ana just stared with her mouth open. Finally she managed, "What? How?"

"Weeellll," Tiffany drawled, always ready for a dramatic storytelling, "The volunteer banquet, you know, was while you were away. And Rita Maynard came! Head volunteer for the whole chain—or whatever you call it, group—of hospitals, statewide, showed up! And brought that! They let me give it to you on account of being your best friend. And your newest recruit to here at the hospital, and all." She took a noisy slurp of her soda. "And Rita told the story of your idea."

"My—what—my idea?"

"About the Listeners. They adopted it statewide. And it's working. She had all kinds of data, about nurses and efficiency and burnout; about patient satisfaction and length of hospitalization and lowered infection rates, all this stuff. Very impressive. We were all so proud of you. I think, if you don't want to put this at home, you know, because you live alone, I think we should display this right by the desk you work at in the ER. On a shelf! In a case! With a light." Finally Tiffany began to eat, and Ana had a moment to think.

Over two years ago, on a whim, she submitted an idea to the employee suggestion box for a Listener. She had, literally, dreamt it up. She'd had a dream that the hospital created a position, several for every shift, a professional whose job it was to listen to patients. Each admitted patient was assigned someone to come sit with them twice a day for half an hour, and listen. The idea was that patients didn't always feel listened to by medical staff. In her dream, a man who'd been mistakenly scheduled for a heart stress test, when he was to go in for a bypass the next day, told his listener who told the nurse that he knew he wasn't to have the test. The nurse called the surgeon who called the on-call cardiologist and the man's life was saved. Ana knew in her dream the test would have killed him. She could *feel* his stress level rising when he tried to tell the tech who came to get him for the test. But his Listener walked in just then and really *listened*. She woke up and thought about how, as a young mother in the Army hospital where she'd had Robin, she had felt so alone, with her family thousands of miles away in Florida and Frank as new to parenthood as she was. She'd choked back tears every time she thought about taking her new baby home and how Frank's CO promised to send him off on maneuvers as soon as the baby was born. Which he did. Even though Ana and Robin had five days in the hospital, she'd never felt so alone in her life. What if she'd had a Listener?

"Well, better late than never," Ana muttered.

"What?"

"Oh, nothing. I was just thinking it would have been nice to have a Listener when I was in the hospital, nineteen years old, not a soul who cared about me within three thousand miles. Frank was sent on maneuvers and then into action in Grenada."

"I know, right? I think Listeners is a terrific idea. And Rita said they are putting them in ERs, too. They can handle all those pesky things you have to chase down nurses for; warm blankets, ice chips if they're allowed, checking to see if family is in the waiting room. And the bigger stuff! Listening to you when you say, that doctor missed what I said about my last surgery! Or, my nurse gave me the stink eye when I asked her to wash her hands, and it says right on that sign to ask your medical professionals to wash their hands! Anyway, congratulations! Sounds like your idea is paying off for the hospitals. They've gotten some attention from competitive medical facilities and there was some article written up in a journal. Good on you, Ana. I don't know where you come up with this stuff."

"I dreamed it."

Tiffany laughed. "Here. Let's take this blueberry pie back to the locker room. I'll take your trophy in my purse and carry the pie, you grab a couple of cups of coffee."

Walking back to the locker room Ana had the strangest feeling. It was as if the life she so carefully planned was slipping away. Like she was in a carnival funhouse trying to navigate between mirrors and the floor was tilting backwards, forwards, sideways; with no warning which way it would go next. She knew a normal person would be happy about the trophy, happy to have an idea produce good results, happy to have a friend. Happy to have blueberry pie, and a good son asking to have her live near; but Ana felt everything slipping away, distorting, refracting. She knew she was anything but normal.

That afternoon at the gym Ana pushed herself, hard. She did over an hour on the treadmill, treated herself to a burrito at a taco shack in the student union, and went back to the gym and swam laps until she felt like her arms were rubber bands. After a shower she sat in the whirlpool, then she drank about a gallon of water from the fountain and showered again. She went back to the hospital instead of all the way out to Haven Beach and crashed again in the locker room before her evening shift in the ER. She had told Tiffany to take the trophy home and figure out where in the hospital, and how, to display it. Ana felt completely out of whack.

The weather turned cool. Ana brought back a soft, thick sweater—a forest green pullover with a rolled collar—from Washington. She had to start thinking about Asheville; she'd be spending Christmas with Ella and her family as usual. She only had two weeks to get her head together and no time for her e-bay business this time of year. It was all she could do to get gifts together for Ella's family and something for Tiffany between her volunteer jobs. She'd done her shopping and wrapping for Robin, Marie and the boys in Washington and left their gifts there. It was a good thing she didn't take classes Fall semester, she had so little time. She broke her light travel rule at Christmas and actually checked a suitcase full of gifts, but usually came home with just her backpack. Just as she did in Washington, she kept a supply of winter clothes at Ella's.

The Monday before she left for Asheville, Tiffany was taking her to the airport on Wednesday, Ana had servicemen coming to the beach house all day. She had the chimney checked for cracks as she did every year and a crew came to take down and store the removable hurricane shutters. Another crew was on the roof blasting it clean with a power washer. After that they did the driveway and garage floor. It was a noisy day. After all of that Ana went over the house with a fine-toothed comb, sprucing up and doing a deep clean, even setting out strings of lights around the windows upstairs and wrapping the porch railing and the stair rail with tinsel. Even though she wouldn't be here for Christmas she wanted the house to have a Christmas feel. She hung fresh wreaths she'd made from cuttings from the tree sale in the library parking lot, striping them with thick red ribbon. She put boughs on the window sills in every room, and they scented the house. She knew the smell would linger and she could just toss them in the trash when she came back two weeks after New Year's. She was staying extra-long in Asheville this year. She wondered as she did these homey chores if this would be her last year in this house; maybe next year she would be helping Robin and Marie decorate before boarding a longer flight—from Seattle to Asheville. She didn't feel any closer to a decision than she had the day Robin and Marie brought it up. But, oddly, she didn't feel stressed or rushed about it. Ana had a feeling she would know the right thing to do when it was the right time to do it.

It had taken about a week but Ana lost her frightening fun-house feeling once she got back into her routines in Robinson. She hoped it would not return when she got back from Asheville; she'd be even busier then since the new semester started the next week. As usual she'd signed up for a Monday night class and a Thursday night class. Things were particularly busy at church the last couple of weeks, with Christmas pageant rehearsals before Sunday night services and after Wednesday prayer meetings. The church kitchen was messier than usual with all the frantic comings and goings, and the fellowship hall had been a mess of tinsel and hay and angel robes and wings. It was odd to be a part of preparations for events she never saw, but Ana remained quietly in the background keeping the younger children sated with grape Kool-aid and daisy cookies, the adults energized with strong coffee and doughnuts. She always stayed late and made sure the kitchen and hall were tided for whatever the next day might bring, and she usually was doing that alone because everybody else was simply done in following service, dinner, then rehearsal.

Tiffany drove Ana to the airport. Ana was quiet as usual. Tiffany, on the other hand was much quieter than normal. Finally, a few miles from the airport, she broke the silence.

"Ana, I'll plan to pick you up on the thirteenth. You have my number, right? If anything changes? I want to tell you, though, there is a possibility I might not be available. I'll let you know of course!"

" Thank you Tiffany." Ana looked over in the surreal glow of the instrument panel at Tiffany's face. Watched her nervous thumbs click back and forth on the wheel, long nails rhythmically tapping.

"Well, and I'm not going to go deeply into this, I'm just telling you in case I end up being unavailable. I know you like privacy and I try to respect that, but I have to breach privacy and bring you inside the situation. So you know if I' m not available,—I'm sorry—why. Edgar is sick. Really, really sick. It's pancreatic cancer. We've known for a while, about three months. I'm okay with it, really I am. He's chosen, and I think it's the right choice, to only treat the pain, not to attempt anything radical. What's keeping him alive basically is the upcoming vote the week following the mayoral election. You probably know nobody's running against him. His singular goal is to make that vote, to leave it as his legacy." Ana saw her dash away one tear under each eye with her sharp, manicured left thumb nail. She waited.

"If something happens\while you're in North Carolina, I might be—unavailable. I'm so sorry." Ana reached over and placed her left hand on Tiffany's shoulder, gave it a squeeze. She realized, distractedly, that it was the first time she'd reached out to touch someone, other than her children and grandchildren, in almost four years.

"This vote is keeping Edgar alive. He wants to make certain that all the dangerous elements, that's what he calls them, *dangerous elements,* are barred from town once and for all, and his is the deciding vote on the city commission. The vice mayor would slide into his seat once he.....once he's gone; Edgar isn't sure how she'd vote, she's a bit of a wild card. An independent. The election is in four weeks, and the vote is the following— his doctors give Edgar at least a couple of more months, so we're not worried. We're having the time we need, I suppose. I'm not good at this but I am doing my best. He hasn't always been the best husband, all those affairs when we were younger were torture,"—Ana had no idea what she was talking about—"and we haven't been in love for years, but it's hard. It's really, really hard."

"I'm sorry, Tiffany." Ana was silent a moment, weighing if she had anything she could offer. After all, she'd been through almost exactly this. How do you prepare someone for widowhood? The truth was, Ana knew, you don't. It was like sex, or childbirth: there was no way to describe it to the unexperienced. She might, however, be able to help after. But could she afford to do that? Could she risk getting that close? Maybe not. The ironic thing was, if Ana chose to take Robin and Marie up on their offer, she could then risk being a real friend to Tiffany. But she'd be gone. Long distance. She thought about how people never really knew each other. She knew most "friends" would be upset, hurt, that they hadn't been brought into the loop on such an important concern. Ana was merely relieved. It also gave her a glimpse into Tiffany's deep respect for Ana's own reserve.

Ana decided on what seemed a safer topic than death. "What dangerous elements?"

"All the people who supposedly move down here for the weather." Ana could see that her distraction technique was working. Tiffany's eyes sparkled not with tears but with humor, the corner of her mouth wrinkled up.

"Oh. Snowbirds. Edgar thinks snowbirds are dangerous?"

Tiffany chuckled. "Oh, Ana. You're so funny. You should know what I'm talking about, being a social work major and all. The bums. The homeless. Edgar was behind that movement a couple of years ago to try to privatize Riverview Drive, you know. The residents who paid big bucks for houses looking out on the Intercoastal and the mangroves got sick of looking at all the boats parked off the channel. People living in the river for free, while we pay the most unGodly property taxes. It just made Edgar's ears smoke that they get the same view free of charge. He put two concrete statues of cannon in the front yard, pointed at the river. I hate those ugly things. The cannons, not the boats.

"Anyhow, there was no way to privatize the road. And I'm glad they didn't, between you and me. Sometimes I look out at those boats and think, *isn't that a better way to live?* Edgar thinks the boat squatters are irresponsible, that they dump waste in the river and stuff, but I've seen most of them motor over to the city marina to fill their water tanks and use the dump station. I think it's a little hypocritical for him to think it is perfectly fine to keep our sailboat—which we have used exactly twice in the past two years—all gassed and ready at our own private dock and think nothing of using the Intracoastal as his own little waterway, and get mad at the boat-dwellers. There's one guy." Tiffany chuckled, and Ana noticed her left hand was now easy on the steering wheel, and she was talking with her right, "This one fellow uses two pool noodles and a Frisbee as his *tender!* He'll zip up one of those soft-sided, floating coolers, loop it around one shoulder and across his chest, and just pool noodle and Frisbee his way over to his boat! I guess he doesn't worry about bull sharks."

"So what is this vote about?"

"Oh, it's to add a statute that law enforcement—land or water—can stop anyone and if they don't have ten dollars to show, and an I.D. with a valid address, a person can be picked up for vagrancy. It'd be pretty easy to clean out the boat dwellers then. And the land-living homeless people, too. It would be up to the cops who to pick up, but it's pretty easy to spot the homeless. And the University is inside the city limits; I've heard lots of people who shouldn't use the library and the all-night study hall. Anyhow, it's pretty much a done deal. Leave it to Edgar, he found a way. But I'll be sad to see the boats go. I think they add to, not take away. Here we are."

They pulled up in front of the departing flights doors. Ana got out, got her pack from the back seat. Tiffany walked around the front of the car. Ana could see that talking about Edgar had backfired; Tiffany was tearing up again. Ana set the pack down between her feet, and reached out for Tiffany and gave her a hard hug. Tiffany's shoulders and back felt as hard as oak. She was a 5'7" plank of tension. When Ana took her by the shoulders and looked in Tiffany's eyes, she realized how haunted the other woman was. "I," Ana said, "am here for you, too. Call me if you need me."

Chapter 14

When Tiffany picked up Ana, Ana was surprised to see she looked better than when she drove her to the airport almost a month before. "I'm so glad to see you Ana! I want to hear all about Ella and her family. I hope I get to meet her soon," Tiffany said as she opened the back door of the Lexus for Ana to throw in her pack.

"I hope you had a good flight. Edgar's death was quite a shock, but I'm doing okay. The funeral is Saturday and the children, thank God, have handled all the arrangements."

"I'm sorry you lost Edgar before he had a chance to see that vote through you were talking about." Ana replied.

"Well, I didn't tell you on the phone, but we came up with a rather creative solution. It was so strange to have him pass away on election day! There was just no time to prepare! An allergic reaction to pain meds! What a shock. I wasn't with him. Riley, our oldest, had taken him to the oncology center at the hospital for his medicine. There was nothing they could do. All considered, it was probably better than what he would have suffered the next couple of months. Ana, are you tired?"

"Not particularly."

"Well, do you mind if I make a stop in town? There's a meeting I have to pop into about this City Commission vote tomorrow. Will you go with me? It's at the Jr. Women's club. I need to run in and tell them something; I don't have to stay for the whole meeting. You can wait for me, it won't take long."

"No, but can we run by the post office on the way in? I'd like to get my mail."

Tiffany glanced at her watch. "Sure."

Ana loved the little beachside post office. The old-fashioned postal clerk's window was closed but the front door was always unlocked and Tiffany waited in the car while Ana went in for her mail. There was only one item—a postcard from Catherine. It had a picture of a snowman made of sand, with seashell buttons, eyes, nose, and mouth, captioned **Christmas in Florida: BRRRRR! Wish you were here.** Ana flipped it to the back.

Hi Ana,

Sorry to have missed you, but hope your Christmas was terrific. We had a nice one and the deep clean is done. Took down the decorations. They were wonderful as usual. Rented to a family from Michigan for all of January and February! Have come up with some terrific ideas for titles for when you worked for me for your resume, call me and we'll discuss.

Love,

Catherine

Ana tucked the card in her pocket as she climbed into the Lexus then put on her seatbelt. Tiffany drove back over the bridge and turned north on Riverside Drive and drove the two short blocks to the Women's Club.

Ana loved the beautiful old building which housed the club; she had walked by several times and looked in the wide casement windows at the old-fashioned auditorium with wooden seats on oak flooring, at the high, stamped-tin ceilings. The only room unviewable from the outside was the kitchen which was off to the left of the raised, curtained stage. She knew this because through the windows she had seen the word *kitchen* on a door, stage right.

"This won't take too long, Ana."

"That's fine. Do you think I could go inside and have a look at the kitchen while you're there? I've always wanted to see it."

"Of course! I'll park around back, behind the auditorium. There's a door there. It leads backstage and also to the kitchen. Both are as gorgeous as the rest of the building. You should look around backstage, too."

It was just sunset when Tiffany parked in the small dark lot behind the large building. There were a half dozen cars; mostly late-model, high-end ones like Tiffany's, in the lot. Ana could smell low tide on the river two blocks away and wondered if the docks under the bridge there were full of evening fishermen. She might walk down there first.

"Tiffany, I've really missed being near the water. I think I'll walk down to the river first if we have time."

"Oh, Ana, I'm really only going to be five minutes. The meeting is in the foyer but I'll take you through the kitchen first and turn on the backstage lights. Can you go down to the river after? I'll go with you."

Ana was a little puzzled but replied, "sure," and followed Tiffany to the backstage door. She opened it, flipped on some lights. Ana could hear a shuffling of feet and murmur of voices which sounded like a lot more than a few people in a foyer, but the acoustics in the auditorium had to be pretty acute. Maybe the sound was just amplified across the empty room. "The kitchen's through there," Tiffany pointed, and disappeared through the drawn stage curtains.

Ana walked into an old-fashioned, beautiful kitchen which faced the shadows cast by the on-ramp to the high-span south bridge, and the parking spots for the fishermen under it. There was a wide oak kitchen table like from a farmhouse country kitchen in the corner of the room with eight chairs around it. In one sat Ana's son, Robin.

For a moment, Ana just stared at Robin, confused. Ana felt a surge of panic, "Robin! What are you doing here? Is something wrong?"

Robin rose, a worried frown wrinkling his forehead. When he was worried he looked just like Frank. "No mom, I just wanted to surprise you. Everything's okay except, well, I hate to tell you this now, I wanted this all to be a great surprise, but I stopped off at the house to drop my bags and *some other family is living there! In the Haven Beach house!* Mom, I don't know what is going on but I think someone is squatting in the house. They were from Michigan and seemed to think I was crazy, said they rented it for all of January! Rented it! Your house! I'd have called the police and tried to straighten it out but I had to be here by 7:45, I promised Tiffany," –how did Robin know Tiffany?—"and besides, I figured you might have sold the house or something without telling me and Ella, but, I'm worried about it. Well, no time to explain now. You're going to have to get out there in a minute, and I promised Tiffany I'd prepare you. I know you've had some public speaking experience lately, with your Volunteer of the Year award in September, and Public Citizen of the Year for the local chapter of the National Assn. of Social Workers last month, but I thought I should spend a few minutes preparing you. It is so wonderful. Ella and I are proud, real proud. Tiffany called us both last week. She seems okay. Reminds me of Aunt Midgie, but not. I think there's more to Tiffany than meets the eye and Midgie is shallow as a Petrie dish."

"Robin! What honor? I don't know what you're talking about."

"Mom. Sit down." Ana sat. " When Mr. Anderson died on election day, the city commissioners got together with the vice mayor, who didn't want the job and filled in for the last week. You're the new mayor. The town wrote you in and the turnout was spectacular. Robinson loves you, mom, and Tiffany is so happy, she is sure you are the perfect person to cast that swing vote tomorrow her husband was so worried about. She's a good friend to you, Mom. Now I guess you have to stay here, but we can just hang onto the apartment for you to use whenever you want and keep coming to visit in the summer."

Ana had known something was coming, she'd felt it. The way she felt a hurricane when she was a child, long before "weatherman" became "meteorologist." She felt hollow, frightened, sick. Then the door opened and Tiffany and Dr. Brewster walked through.

"Ana," Tiffany said as she pulled out a chair and sat down, taking Ana's hands in hers. Dr. Brewster leaned against the door to the auditorium, watching Ana. "Now, don't be mad. It made so much sense. I know you will vote your conscious, and I know you are as worried about the influx of homeless—even boat squatters in the Waterway—as I am, as Edgar was. There's not a person in this town who would disagree with you for mayor, you were really the only choice for write in. All you have to do is come out and accept. Say a little something. A lot of the town is out there. All the other volunteers from the hospital and library, the people from your church. Robin here didn't know you were working on a degree, I kind of let that cat out of the bag, but for the town it's—perfect! You'll represent what is best about our town and serve it so well. Please say yes."

Sorry, Brewster mouthed.

Ana just stood up, walked through the stage door, and climbed the steps stage right in front of the curtain. She heard the others follow her through. Tiffany proudly passed her and smiled at the thundering crowd. Finally everyone who could took their seats. The street doors were wide open. Ana could see the Emergency Room sign glowing in the twilight across the hospital parking lot next door.

"Everyone! Please! Sit down. It is my great honor," Tiffany crooned into the microphone, "to introduce to you the write-in mayor-elect of Robinson, the person so perfect to carry out Edgar's legacy. She has been briefed on her surprise election and is well rested to sit for the City Commission meeting tomorrow, to vote regarding the barring of homeless persons from use of services or sheltering inside the Robinson city limits on land or water. May I introduce Haven Beach Resident, Ana Mills!"

Ana was clenching and unclenching her hands at her sides as Tiffany spoke. She abstractly looked down and noticed that she had managed to wrinkle the unwrinklable material of her paisley dress. She'd been grasping it. Slowly she opened her hands and let go. She noticed Robin and Dr. Brewster take two seats obviously held for them right in front of the podium. She chose, as she stood behind the podium and took the stem of the microphone in one hand, to look not at Robin but straight at Dr. Brewster's face. She thought again about the distances between people. She realized that no matter how carefully you held yourself it is impossible to love but not to hurt the ones you love. Ana knew now was the time to share her secret. As she realized it she felt herself relax, her stomach settle. It seemed that of its own accord her backbone straightened and she stood taller. She didn't know what she would do after she spoke but she knew the right thing to say. Maybe she'd leave with Robin when he went back to Bellingham. Maybe she would have a frank talk with Dr. Brewster, finish her degree, and stay here.

"Hello. First I want to thank you for this honor. I had no idea..." Ana paused and drew breath, "no idea I had so many friends. This is of course a great honor and one, as I will explain, I must pass by." Ana looked down and waited for the shocked murmuring to stop. She didn't dare look at Tiffany. "You see, Mrs. Anderson misunderstands something. It isn't her fault. I'm a registered Democrat," there was polite laughter, some clapping, "I registered when I first moved here four years ago and was staying at the Bella Vista Inn. That address is still on my voter registration, and my license."

"A minor problem we can fix!" called Tiffany. Laughter and more clapping followed.

"Actually Tiffany, no we can't." Ana looked at Dr. Brewster, and was relieved to see his steady eyes register no surprise as she said, "because I don't live at Haven Beach. I live *on Haven Beach*. I'm homeless."

Dr. Brewster, without rising from his seat, slowly began to clap. The sound echoed eerily in the old room, beyond the collective gasp. It was the last thing Ana heard as she walked into the kitchen, picked up her pack, and carefully opened the door to the outside.

NOTES

Page 4.

Usually when Ana Ana (Therill) Mills is 58 years old. She was born in Gainesville, Florida on October 6th, 1956. She grew up in Flagler Beach, Florida, the fourth of five children. Her mother was an avid reader, volunteer at the local library, and chair of the visitation committee at the First Baptist Church. Ana was baptized on Mother's Day, 1964. The Therill family attended church on Sunday mornings for Sunday school and worship service, Sunday evening, and Wednesday night for prayer meeting throughout Ana's childhood. Her father was Sunday School director and chair of the finance committee. He was from Grenada, Mississippi, an orphan who earned a degree in civil engineering from Georgia Tech through the Navy ROTC program. He worked for a surveying company in Jacksonville, Florida after the Navy, where he met Ana's mother. When Ana was four years old he went to work for NASA. Ana didn't know what he did for a living but she got to watch all the launches at Cape Canaveral from the VIP stands with her mother, brothers, and sisters.

Ana met Frank Mills in drama class their sophomore year in high school. He liked her long blond hair and used to sit behind her and play with it. They married when he graduated from high school; Frank did three years in the Army—their son was born in an Army hospital— then went to work for the Florida East Coast Railroad, later for Amtrak. He was a station manager, and transferred to New Jersey. Their daughter Ella was born five years later. Ana stayed home with the children. After Frank died she moved to the town of Robinson, Florida, forty miles south of Flagler Beach.

Sure enough, even Judee Marquetta Golden is 36 years old. She is a single mother, never married, of two teenaged girls. She has been a nurse for five years, having worked nights as a certified nursing assistant at a nursing home to put herself through nursing school. Her fourteen year old daughter is mildly mentally handicapped and three months pregnant by someone she met at the all-children's playground. Judee is a Robinson native, born in the hospital she works at. She doesn't vote or care about politics but she is deathly afraid of men and of sharks. She doesn't swim and she doesn't date. Her oldest daughter is the result of a gang rape at a frat house party.

Judee turned back Billy Everett Preston 11, is an honor roll fifth grader at Ponce DeLeon Elementary in Haven Beach. He has a big brother who is on the high school basketball team. Billy has red hair and freckles and his ears stick out. His parents won't let him wear his hair long enough to cover them, so he wears a baseball cap whenever possible. He sleeps in a baseball cap in hopes that it will move his ears closer to his head. He gets teased at school, called Billy Billy Big Ears. His hero is his big brother who got him the job as water-boy for the football team. They let him wear a ball cap to all the games. He has a secret crush on a girl in his class named Brooklyn who wears combat boots and long skirts year-round. She is skinny and has an auditory processing deficit so she never says anything in class and has to sit next to the teacher's desk.

Her favorite was John (no middle name) Clinton, 68, is a retired astrophysicist from New Mexico who moved to Robinson six years ago. After the desert, Robinson seemed impossibly crowded and close. He bought a good camera and started taking pictures of things which bothered him, like SUV's and trucks and recyclables in garbage cans. Once he began to feel a part of the town and to accept it he started taking pictures of flora unfamiliar from his past life in New Mexico. He is particularly fond of photographing live oak trees. He lives with his life-partner in a condo in Haven Beach, a retired army colonel named Casey Lovett. They enjoy walking the beach at low-tide with a garden trowel and metal detector. The most interesting thing they had found, so far, is a World War Two era Nazi wristwatch inscribed, Hauptmann, *Stumm, unter, und tödlich, Ihr Führer.*

Page 5.

Ana kept one Frank Marcus Mills (deceased) was born in 1955 in Kenosha, Wisconsin, the middle child of Lee and Sarah (Clancy) Mills. He was raised Catholic and as the second son was expected to go into the priesthood. When his parents moved to the Florida coast Frank was fourteen. His father was part of a new real estate venture seeking to aggressively convert the small town of Flagler Beach to a wealthy retirement destination for northerners. Frank's mother's role was to run a wine and cheese store catering to these clients. The store was only partially successful; the Mills' hadn't counted on the tea-totaling nature of the local population. After their children were grown they retired to coastal Maryland, finding the Florida summers increasingly brutal.

Frank fell in love with Ana Therill the first time he saw her walking down the beach in a brown and white cotton bikini which was too big in the butt and threatened to fall off every time she walked from the dune line to the water. He also fell in love with the ocean and collected soda bottles and mowed lawns to buy his first surfboard. Frank shared a bedroom with his brother, and one evening as they were falling asleep, Montgomery described in horrible detail a sexual encounter he had with a thirteen year old boy, a runaway, in Jacksonville Beach the previous night. Frank punched his brother in the mouth, got dressed and grabbed his wallet, climbed out the bedroom window, took his surfboard from the side of the house and went down to the beach. The next morning, Frank went to a phone booth and made an anonymous call to the department of children and families reporting what his brother had done. He camped under the boardwalk and the following Monday enlisted in the Army. He never told anyone else what his brother had done, but he also never spoke to Montgomery again.

Frank married Ana and they had two children. He was eleven years short of retirement when he got sick and lost his job with the railroad. He had recently been converted to part-time but never told his wife. His death by Huntington's ate up all savings and assets which were in his own name.

Page 6.

There were some Margaret Bridgett (McNaulty) Phillips is 67 years old, and had married at eighteen her high school sweetheart, Roberto in Charleston, South Carolina. She worked as an eighth grade science teacher at a private school; he was the custodian there. Both wanted children, but they were unable to have them. When they were sixty-two Roberto and Margaret retired to Robinson. Roberto spent his days fishing in a john boat on the Intracoastal Waterway. Margaret does cross stitch, watches soap operas on television, and volunteers three afternoons a week at the hospital. She fell in love and began a flirtation, what she hoped would turn into an affair, with Roger Ahern, a widower from Monterey, California.

Roger Ryan Ahern 83, is a north California native who worked in the canneries from the time he dropped out of high school at fifteen until he was seventy-two years old. He is six foot five, weighs three hundred pounds. Powerful as a young man, all his muscle had gone to fat as soon as he left the cannery. Roger is a gregarious octogenarian who likes the ladies and has twin daughters, Breck and Brock, in the Navy. They will both reach retirement in three years and his secret dread is that they retire to Robinson. He collects postage stamps and spends his free time and his saving studying for and traveling to philatelic conventions and auctions. He is fond of Mrs. Phillips but has no intention of entering into a relationship with her outside of joking around when on duty at the hospital. He volunteers because he swore he would to his dying wife, who passed away at the Robinson hospital of a burst appendix five years ago.

Page 7.

"Andy McNamara," replied Andrew Elvis MacNamara IV, 47. He served his country as a CIA agent based in Langley, Virginia for fourteen years, joining the agency immediately after receiving a master's in psychology from Harvard University at 23 years old. He came from a long line of patriots; both of his parents were eastern bloc spies during the Cold War. His grandfather was a Navy flyer killed in the raid on Tokyo following the attack on Pearl Harbor. Andy has foregone family life and friendship for service to his country. In an undercover job in 2005 he failed to notice an asset slipping a powerful drug into his drink at a crucial moment; the mistake resulted in the deaths of three agents. Andy lost his job and climbed into a bottle; he eventually was evicted from his apartment and began walking toward Florida with a vague notion of suicide in Key West as the sun sunk beneath the horizon and the revelers around him cheered. He planned to swim until he sank.

The security guard Terrell Elias Realmuto, 39, works two jobs; as a cop in Port Orange and as security guard at the hospital. He and his wife, Earline, live with Terrell's mother in West Robinson. They have two children in college, boys, at Florida State. Both won scholarships for baseball. One is a pitcher, the other a catcher. Terrell works so much that he only has time for one hobby—he belongs to a hunt club where he hunts wild pigs with nothing but a bowie knife. He goes on four hunts a year and bags a hog every time. Terrell drinks Miller High Life and falls asleep in front of the television on his rare days off.

Page 8

At that moment Lynn Thomas Till, 17, has Asperger's syndrome. The thing he wants most in the world is friends so he learned to surf. He read everything he could about surfing and surfers and sat on the beach and watched for three years before trying it. He has perfect technique, and can't understand why the other surfers his age laugh at him or yell at him no matter what he does or says. He heard some boys he knew from school arguing that nobody was brave enough to night surf in these shark-infested waters, so Lynn said, "I will." The event was scheduled for Friday night. All the boys showed up to watch; there was a full moon. Several girls showed up too, which Lynn hadn't expected. Two of them, the Johnston twins Jessica and Jenna, begged him not to go out. He got nipped by something after his first ride, close to shore. Jessica and Jenna drove him to the hospital, followed by a jeep full of boys.

Page 9

For instance, when Robin George Mills, 37, was named after a Carly Simon song his mother heard in junior high school, *His friends are more than fond of Robin,* and his great uncle George on his father's side. Like his father was, he is a railroad man. His wife is from Bellingham, Washington and loves to hike. Robin loves it too. They camped and hiked nearly every weekend, barely breaking stride for the birth of their twin boys, Lucas and Sam. They took the boys on their first camping trip on Mt. Ranier at two months of age. Lucas and Sam love the outdoors, and plan to be National Park rangers after completing college. They are in their first year of environmental sciences at Western Washington University and living at home. Robin and his wife, Marie, were planning their first trip without the boys by asking his mother to stay with them in November. Robin and Marie were doing a Rocky Mountain Special trip, eight days. Robin has a secret only his wife, doctor, mother, father and sister know about, and which he despises; webbed toes. He plans to have them surgically corrected when his sons go for Junior year abroad.

Page 10

They were a Ella Miriam Mills, 33, was named after her mother's great grandmother and Moses' sister from the Bible. Ella married Julian, whom she met in high school. They married the day after graduation, both having gotten into Warren Wilson College in Swannanoa, North Carolina. They got an apartment close to campus, borrowed the maximum in student loans, then worked as teachers and participated in the public service loan forgiveness program to pay off the loans. Ella had their first child, Elise, during summer break between freshman and sophomore year. She and Julian managed their classes for the next three years so that one of them was always home with the baby whose sister Casey arrived just thirteen months later. They were one of only three married couples in which both partners were students. After graduation Julian went immediately to work at a local middle school teaching English; when Casey went to Kindergarten, Ella took a job at the elementary school teaching fifth grade. They are die-hard lefties. Both play the dulcimer. It secretly bothers Ella that Elise in particular shows signs of being at least mildly conservative. She hasn't shared this fear with Julian, but noticed that Elise tends to date boys with very short hair who play football.

Page 12

The loneliness, missing Russell Ryan Therrill, 63, lives in Raleigh, North Carolina. He is a chemist who owns his own consulting firm, the oldest of five siblings, Ana's oldest brother. He is married to Daisy Ames who also holds a PhD from Florida State University. She works at Duke University. They have no children. Russell and Lisa love to travel and have visited six of the seven continents. They are working on eating at every one of a particular chain of seafood restaurants; when they do, the will be rewarded with a trip around the world.

David John Therrill, 57, has never married. He is a writer living in a cabin outside Kallispell, Montana. He loves getting postcards from his sister Ana and uses them as the basis for most of his short stories. He keeps them tacked to a wall in his one-room cabin, over his desk.

Sara Louise Therrill Broadhurst, 53, lives with her husband Hugh in Atlanta, Georgia. They have two adopted daughters, Joan and Jane. The girls attend Vanderbilt and have an apartment off campus. They love hiking with their cousins in Asheville. Sara is a state representative and has a practice in environmental law. Her husband is a carpenter.

Mary Therrill, 51, sculptor living in Chicago with her husband of thirty years, Theodore Minton. Theodore runs a small blues club and Mary, who plays piano, sometimes fills in. Theo is a Vietnam veteran and is highly regarded for his kindness to others; over the club is an apartment where he has been known to quietly assist fellow veterans who need a hand.

Beulah Bonita Campbell Therrill, deceased. Ana's mother, known as Miss Bea, was the town librarian in Flagler Beach when Ana was a girl. Most of Ana's friends' mothers didn't work, and Miss Bea worked out her schedule at the library so that she arrived home just a quarter of an hour after the children got home from school. From the time Ana was a little girl she would enter the house and rush from room to room, making beds and opening windows to air the rooms as soon as she got home. She set the breakfast dishes soaking, quickly hung the morning wash, wiped down the table and washed the dishes before her mother got home. She loved the relief on her mother's face when she opened the front door, took a deep breath, and let her shoulders sag. "Oh," Ana's mother would say, "I can take a nap." She never asked which of her children did the chores, and from her childhood on Ana associated a clean house with taking a nap, something she herself loved to do. Miss Bea was a petite, pretty blond. Both Sara and Mary very much resembled their mother. She came from a large Charleston family; her great-grandfather fought with Marion the Swamp Fox.

Roscoe Russell Therill, deceased. Russ Therill, fondly called R.T. by his coworkers, was orphaned at age six when both of his parents were killed in a tornado in Greenville, Mississippi. They were visiting his mother's brother, who was also killed. Russ was raised by various relatives during the Depression. He took the Navy ROTC exam his senior year of high school, taking the train to New Orleans with his best friend, Mark Sheffield. They took it on a dare by a classmate. Both passed and both attended Georgia Tech, studying Civil Engineering. After paying back the Navy for his scholarship with six years of duty, Russ went to work for NASA at Redstone Arsenal in Alabama. He was transferred to Cape Canaveral as soon as the facility was completed. He loved designing rockets and felt he led a magical life. He was a deacon at the First Baptist of Flagler Beach. He passed away of a heart attack two weeks after his wife died of a stroke. He was seventy-four.

Ana had always Memory Mae Lipsey, 74, was born in Grenada Mississippi and has never been out of the state. She works at Mo' Suga' on Thursday nights, only. The rest of the time she bakes fresh pies for the restaurant. She uses the money from this income to support orphan children through the

Christian Children's Fund. Memory collects stamps and coins. One of her favorite things to do in her free time is exchange rolled coins at the bank and go home to go through them for rare ones. She was very disappointed by the state quarters series, and is hopeful that Rosa Parks gets put on the new twenty dollar bill.

Page 13

At first, when

James Harlan Mills, deceased. James was the youngest of five brothers and grew up in Bemidji, Minnesota. He hated snow and vowed to live in Florida as an adult. He left high school a semester early after completing vocational training in building and repairing boat engines. He eloped with his girlfriend, Sara Snodgrass, and they moved to Florida. James and Sara went back and forth from Florida to Minnesota for all the first thirty years of their marriage. He repaired boat engines when they lived in Minnesota, but in Florida sold real estate. He, like both of his parents, was Catholic and was also an alcoholic. He died of acute liver failure in 1994.

Sara Snodgrass Mills, deceased. Sara grew up an only child in Bemidji, Minnesota. She came from a teatotalling Lutheran family, and remained a teatotaler herself all her life even though she owned a wine and cheese shop in Florida. When her husband died Sara sold her shop and moved to Maryland to be closer to her grandchildren.

Montgomery Sheldon Mills, 63. Montgomery lives in Meridian, Mississippi. He is married to Slua Starkey, 61. The marriage is a front; both Slua and Montgomery are homosexual. She is promiscuous and has partners, but Montgomery lives in a private hell of believing he will go to hell for being gay. Slua is his best friend but doesn't know he feels that way. They raise labradoodles and both work at a slaughterhouse outside of town. Montgomery is pretty much afraid of everything.

Midge Roberta Mills Lister, 58. Midge was given everything she wanted as a child and spoiled rotten. While her brothers were raised with stringent rules and beatings, Midge was treated as a princess by her father, who had grown up with brothers and always wanted a sister. She was allowed to take and break her brothers' toys. When in high school she vowed to marry for money, telling anyone who listened that she could do better than her parents and grandparents had done and didn't mind using her body to do so. Work and childbirth were both beneath her. She vowed never to do either.

Page 24

The note from David Lawrence Brewster, 61, was born and raised in Johnson City, Tennessee. He married his childhood friend and next door neighbor, Regina Wilder. They cannot remember when they didn't know each other. They have four daughters. Regina is a writer and very shy; most people who know Dr. Brewster don't even realize he is married. He has taught at the University in Robinson for thirty-four years, taking the job straight out of graduate school. He and Regina spend a part of each summer hiking a section of the Appalachian Trail. He is outgoing and believes that the most effective change, sociologically, takes place at the local level. He has a reputation for intelligence and deliberate consideration. Even the more conservative politicians in Robinson tend to trust his judgment and vision for the future of the town.

Page 28

Ana looked around Tyler Roakie, 26. Tyler drives a truck which has an interesting modification, it is able to do "rolling coal" basically spraying black smoke in a cloud at the push of a button. He likes to do this to African Americans in cars, on motorcycles, and especially walking down a street. He's an unashamed racist with an I.Q. of 84. It took him eight years to successfully complete three semesters of community college. He has never had a girlfriend and is beginning to take his frustrations out on women, too, with his rolling coal.

Riley Allen Messiner, 22. Riley wants to be a cowboy so he hangs out with Tyler because he drives a truck and lives on a pig farm west of town. Riley is growing more and more disturbed by Tyler's behavior—he has thought of confronting him but knows Tyler has a terrible temper and several guns. Riley is in love from afar with a girl he graduated from high school with, Lisamarie Westheimer.

Page 31

A girl in Lisamarie Westheimer, 21. Lisamarie is working on her Registered Nursing Bachelor's degree and plans to become a Physician's Assistant. She is extremely shy and knows Riley Messiner likes her but doesn't know how to let him know she knows. She just keeps adding classes he is taking to her schedule and hopes he is able to figure it out. She lives at home with her father, who has severe Rheumatoid Arthritis and is confined to a wheelchair. She works at the local McDonald's. They live in Section 8 housing near the university. She has a secret wish to learn to drive and someday have a car so she can quit taking the bus. Her mother and sister died in a car accident when Lisamarie was four.

Page 42

"Ana! How nice Martina Alona Martinez Anderson, 47, has lived in Robinson her whole life. She was born in the hospital she volunteers at. She and her husband have four daughters; all the girls have their mother's curly hair and round figure. Martina is perfectly content with her own looks; she never wears makeup and trims her own hair. She looks forward eagerly to growing old with her husband and is secretly thrilled to find that, after almost thirty years, they have more fun together—in and out of bed—than ever before. She thinks more people should get married young and the world would be a safer, more peaceful place.

Page 44

The owner was David Robert Jackson, 57. David inherited the Bella Vista when he was 18 from his mother, who raised him there by herself. He has never lived anywhere else. He wanted to be a doctor but the motel had been in his family since 1911. He is bitter from watching developers from the north ruin not only the wild spaces in and around Robinson but the character of the town. There are now festivals year-round, and they have not helped his business at all, which is constantly booked due to the time-proven reputation of cleanliness, economy, and privacy, and the beautiful view. Lately he has been fighting aggressive bids to sell backed up by an annoying increase in city inspections.

Page 48

There was a George Mike Vance, 32, is from Waco, Texas, and First Baptist is his first church. He was selected as pastor straight out of graduate school. When he arrived in Robinson he couldn't believe how blessed he was to be called to preach in such a beautiful place. Although he was nervous, he knew God was in control and would guide him. Some of the congregation gave him a difficult time, testing him privately and publicly, he assumed due to his youth. Each evening when he begins his nighttime prayers, he always begins with, "Thank you."

Page 49

It was something Ethel Margaret McKenzie, deceased. Ethel lived her entire life in Atlanta, Georgia. Ana used to take the train to spend a week in summer with her grandmother. Her grandchildren, including Ana, called her "Mother Maggie." Mother Maggie kept a spotless house and loved to cook for her grandchildren even though she herself had no sense of smell and therefore couldn't taste food, either. She was a tiny woman and although an old-fashioned Southern Baptist, loved to dance. She also loved to read and went to the library every week of her adult life and checked out six books, which she read before returning to the library the next week. She was the most literate person Ana ever knew and inspired her love of books.

Page 50

Her first week Patti Ann Partimonious, 32. Patti Ann has four daughters and lost her husband in a construction accident. Neither the Partimonious family nor the employer was insured at the time of the accident, which killed two workers when a crane broke. Patti Ann is a professional on-line shopper, filling orders for local executives while her children are at school. She has a secret desire to try to save some money up to move to Florida, but she can't even afford a car.

Page 51

At the bottom Kyle Edward Tankersley, 50, and Keith Elton Tankersley, 50. The Tankersleys are twins who live together on Staten Island in an apartment in the top floor of an old row house, a block from the ferry.

They work in the Equitable Building on the corner of Broadway and Wall Streets for the Attorney General of New York as investigators. In their work, being identical twins has come in handy. In high school Kyle took all their English classes and Keith all the maths. Nobody every figured it out.

Page 54

When she passed Tiffany Tara Tyler Sullivan, 47 Tiffany grew up in Robinson and is a third-generation realtor. She enjoys her work and has a reputation for honesty. She is married to Edgar Sullivan, 49. Edgar is mayor and Tiffany secretly hates being wife of the mayor and all of the public duties that entails. But she loves Edgar, even though throughout their entire marriage he has had quiet affairs with various city employees. Edgar is on an obsessive mission to get rid of homelessness entirely in Robinson, and Tiffany entirely disagrees with his methods and has a few radical ideas about homelessness and Robinson of her own, which she shares with nobody.

Page 57

I think Gome Laura Luanne Moxley, 59, lives in Opp, Alabama. She works at a Piggly Wiggly and also at a local bar, singing for a rock and roll cover band. In high school in Flagler Beach, she was voted Most Beautiful and Most Likely to Succeed, and was both Prom and Homecoming Queen. She dated David Mills off and on from sixth grade until he left town for college, but her favorite activity in high school had been attempting to make him miserable by flirting with, and sometimes giving blow jobs to, other boys on the beach. David always treated her better than other boys, and resisted her sexual advances. She had wanted them to give each other their virginity and marry, but David knew she would make him miserable and finally broke up with her in eleventh grade.

Page 69

Once a girl Lila Lu Oxtanaria, 64 Lila Lu grew up in Sopchoppy, Florida the daughter of a fisherman and waitress. She skipped two grades and went to Florida State University on a scholarship. She became an epidemiologist and works for the World Health Organization leading research on the effect of global warming on the propagation of new viruses.

Page 75

The lifeguard was Tana Suzanne Rotundo, 16. Tana is captain of the local high school swim team, and was accelerated a grade in school. She works to help her mother support the family. She has six younger sisters; their father left when Tana was 14. She tried out for the local lifeguards two weeks later. Tana is the best lifeguard in the county and has the awards to prove it. She is afraid of nothing on the beach or in the water, but is secretly afraid that if she goes away to college as planned there won't be enough food on the table. She wants to be a doctor.

Page 77

There was always Jennifer Winters, 22 Moved to Robinson from Kenosha, Wisconsin to attend the University. She wants to be a Physician's Assistant but it will take a long time as she attends school half time and works as a waitress to put herself through school. Her parents wanted her to go into the very successful family business, plumbing supplies, so refuse to fill out her financial aid paperwork or to help her in any way with college. She is determined to put herself through, but until she is twenty-six years old students loans will be unavailable to her without her parents' tax return. She volunteers at the hospital and dreams of being a PA.

Page 84

This trip, Ana Julia Minton Morrow, 32. Julia takes three weeks off of her job to spend with her daughter at the end of every August. Her husband is a stay at home dad and she sometimes gets very jealous that he spends so much time with their four children, while she often has to be away. She is an analyst with the World Bank. Julia travels most of the time but tries to manage to spend at least four days at home per month. Sometimes, in summer, her family travels with her. Julia's time in the Keys is her only real experience with community life in Robinson, and it makes her very lonely. She is contemplating quitting her high-paying job but knows her family is used to living on the ocean and having plenty of ready cash. She discusses this with no one.

Page 87

The thought of Catherine Joanne Marantz Hillier, 68. Catherine is a successful businesswoman. She owns laundromats throughout New Jersey. She started with a cleaning service when she was in her twenties to buy a house of her own in Haven Beach. She owns a beach house, which she rents out except for the month of July and Thanksgiving through Christmas. She used to use it in July, but now uses it during the Thanksgiving through Christmas holiday season, when she supervises a deep clean and repairs. Catherine has considered hiring a local real estate office to manage the property, but instead uses her old friend Ana, who keeps it spic and span year round in exchange for use of the property in July.

Page 89

The mate gave Michael Vincent Calhoun, 24. Michael is a native of the Keys, or a Conch. He is very comfortable on the water and in it. A natural sailor, Michael prefers sail over motoring, but is saving money for college by working as a mate for the National Parks Service. He has no intention of going to college, and when he has enough money saved plans to buy his own sloop to live aboard. Michael is terrified of telling his parents, who own a gas station, that he doesn't really want to go to college.

Page 90

When the girls Maya Sally Smith, 14, is scared of water. Her father is a professional treasure hunter and wants Maya to learn to scuba dive to help him. Maya would prefer never to get in a boat and to live in the middle of the Great Plains, or anywhere far from the ocean. Lucinda Bonita Butler, 13, is a vain middle-schooler with what she considers the prettiest hair in town; it is thick, curly and black as a crow's wing. She spends hours poring through fashion magazines, looking for the next hairstyle to best show off her tresses.

Page 92

She was surprised Lita Anne Marquez, 16, is the pampered daughter of Rafael and Jane, who own the most exclusive condominium complex in Robinson. She is fully aware of her privileged position and prefers to spend her time working at the local McDonald's and volunteering as she secretly wants nothing more than to be an ordinary girl with a family that works together to make ends meet. She is very lonely, as most of her childhood was supervised by a series of paid employees while her parents traveled all over the world.

Lita and her Jane Marquez, 41. Jane Marquez has a sweet and giving nature, which she passed on to her daughter. She inherited a large trust from a great aunt when she was 14, and she and her husband invested in condominiums in Robinson. Neither has ever worked. Jane is a bit puzzled that Lita insists on flipping burgers. Jane had four miscarriages before Lita and two after, and secretly wishes she'd had a large family. She's never told Lita about the miscarriages and is struggling with if she should or not.

Page 102

Her great Aunt Sadie Doolittle, deceased. Sadie Doolittle from Meridian, Mississippi didn't marry until she was in her forties and outlived her husband by two decades. After her husband's death Sadie traveled and always traveled light. She had an adventurous spirit which was common in her family. She was a first cousin of Jimmy Doolittle, naval aviator.

Page 115

And Rita Maynard Rita Maynard, 34, is the state of Florida Volunteer of the Year for 2014. She lives in Ocala with her husband, Renard, and owns a horse farm and a chain of mortuaries. She stays extremely active with volunteering because she cannot stand the family business.

How she did it, and why I wrote it

I wrote this book because I've become increasingly concerned regarding the attitudes of those who've never been hungry, never lived on the edge, toward the growing number of citizens who are teetering there or have tumbled over. Recently, in nearby Daytona, citizens put together a homeless shelter where individuals can eat, sleep, and have mental health services. As if homelessness is synonymous with mental illness. As if, as a matter of course, a person wouldn't be homeless without something being wrong with their *mind*. This, and particularly the public's lack of concern with this pairing, is only one indicator of the astonishing bigotry associated with poverty in this nation. Assumptions and misconceptions abound.

Here's another—and for me more personal—example. A friend of mine who for the last six years lived with and assisted her mother was recently named as a beneficiary in her mother's will. My friend doesn't drive or have a job. An executor is in charge of the will. My friend's portion is to go into an irrevocable trust. Her nieces' shares, because they are under twenty-five, go into a separate trust. They have husbands, jobs. She doesn't. Because my friend is without income the executor and other beneficiaries have gotten together, cleaned out the home my friend lives in while ordering her to sit outside, told her how she should spend her trust income, and decided it should be a "special needs" trust. When I pressed them on why "special needs" they shouted at me, *because she doesn't drive. Because she doesn't have a job!* Again, the layers of ignorance are mind-numbing.

In the coastal central Florida town I live in (which the town of Robinson is modeled after) the divide between the haves and have-nots is ever more apparent. Because it is a touristy beach town, restaurants abound. Few offer a living wage to the workers. One restaurant in town offers sick days, retirement, health care benefits. Yet more and more tourists clog the roads, making it harder for locals to get to work. Skateboarding is illegal on our streets: falling down drunk is not. There are all kinds of drunken festivals throughout the year. Wine walks. Bike and bars—ride your bicycle from bar to bar. Supposedly, all of this is good for the town. The truth is the minimum wage and below it jobs, which are on the rise, actually lower the per capita income.

My own situation has ranged greatly over the years—my husband and I raised four sons in a 1,200 square foot home in a working-class neighborhood. While we are fortunate enough to own our home, there have been difficult times. We both hold higher degrees but chose as careers public service. During the housing crisis we fell victim to a predatory lender in a refinancing; the lender actually changed our paperwork after it was signed and notarized from a fixed rate of interest to an adjustable. Although victims eventually won a class-action suit (this was done to hundreds of mortgage holders), instead of surrendering our home to foreclosure we chose to continue paying the mortgage and for years paid over $2,000 a month. Not allowing the house to go to foreclosure during this time was a poor fiscal decision on our part. We know that. However, it was more important to us to raise our sons in one house, in one town, near as many of their grandparents as possible (three of the four lived within ten miles) than to move out of state where we could make a fresh start. We also wanted to model a servant attitude—as I said, we *chose* public service. And this town. And living near our parents. We will never get the money we lost in those years back.

When we had three children in diapers my husband and I sat down and figured out that, after child care and taxes, he was bringing home 29 cents an hour as a firemedic. This was very discouraging for him. We decided that since he was vested, he would leave the fire service and work from home in the private sector to care for the boys while I was teaching. He worked for a brokerage house out of Brooklyn doing online customer support from our home in Florida. One of my brothers, a vice president at the brokerage, got him the job. One year, he made trades as a day-trader with some modest gains. He was good at it. However, his employer criminally reported all of his trades (and those of many other employees) as gains, leaving us with over forty thousand dollars in tax debt. The employer was caught; our tax situation was irreparable. We are still paying for those back taxes. Unfortunately, a few years earlier I'd experienced an emergency brain surgery which took place in the middle of the night on New Year's Eve. Since I was not expected to live financial concerns were the last thing on our minds. While I was literally under the knife (at this time my husband was still a firefighter and I was teaching) our health insurance carrier switched from a PPO to self-insured.

For two years following my surgery the two insurance companies refused to pay the bill which amounted to over $100,000. Each claimed the other was responsible to pay. Finally they agreed to split the bill, but by that time our credit was completely ruined.

Shortly after my husband lost his position with the brokerage our own living was reduced to poverty level. Although we were both working very hard, we could barely keep food on the table. This went on for years. Because we were "poor" relatives politely quit visiting; if family came to town, we met at a restaurant (which we usually could not afford to do.) Distances grew and we were treated with condescension. There were times we could only afford to pay either our power bill or our water bill; sometimes we had to take showers at the public ones at the beach and port drinking and cooking water purchased at the market. We flushed toilets and mopped the floor with rainwater. All while keeping up huge mortgage and tax payments. It was during this time that I began to make note of the razor-thin line between "sheltered" and "homeless."

I also realized how shallow are our perceptions of others. Although I had friends in similar, or worse, financial straits, most of them pretended they were not. They seemed ashamed of and dishonest about their situations. This made me think about the deceptions we foist on each other, even on friends and family. Perhaps that was why—this culture of lies—it seemed easy for my own siblings in particular to ignore a sister and her family living below poverty level.

I was working full-time at the University of Central Florida as a Coordinator of Educational Training Programs at the Center for Autism and Related Disabilities. While I served mainly in the county I lived in, Volusia, once a week I had to drive to Orlando, 115 miles round trip, for a clinical meeting. My husband was at that particular time working on a bachelor's degree. We had three sons living at home; two in high school and one in middle school. Both the middle school boy and the oldest had after-school and weekend jobs as bus boys at a local restaurant; our middle son was attending a rigorous magnet International Baccalaureate program in a neighboring town, so he didn't have a job. He also has the form of autism formerly known as Asperger's as well as arthritis. So, three of us in the home were working at that time. This was after the financial crash and after my husband lost his job at the brokerage. Of twelve remote support personnel, Mikel was the last one to be let go before the job was phased out. At that time he decided to go back to college. His student loans and grants provided some extra income after tuition and fees.

We qualified for both reduced lunches at school for the boys and for government commodities, a very old federal program. Commodities are distributed through local churches. We chose to access the food bank at a church in nearby Port Orange, where our son's magnet school was. Unfortunately distributions took place on Tuesday afternoons, the same day as my clinical meetings in Orlando. My husband was in class on Tuesdays, and took the local bus as we had one vehicle. I would rush from Orlando to make it to Port Orange then stand in line in my suit and heels. The distribution was around the back of the church. The line was generally long. Once patrons retrieved their paperwork from one window, they took it to the next window and handed it over. The person who then checked the paperwork and called instructions to volunteers packing boxes and bags happened to be the pastor's mother, a woman in her late sixties. Every time she spoke to me, after she'd called "Family of five!" to the volunteers, she chatted a bit and always asked, "How's the job search going?" Every single time I told her, "I have a job" she looked puzzled.

One particularly trying afternoon I lost my patience and although I wasn't rude, said, "Listen, I not only work full-time, I have a terminal degree. I teach at UCF."

"A terminal degree? What's that?"

"If it doesn't kill you, you're done."—my standard answer in trying to explain the MFA. She looked blank. "Like….a doctorate. A PhD."

"And you still qualify for free food?"

"Yes, ma'am, check the paperwork."

More puzzlement. "Well, there are four other people in your household. Why don't they have jobs?"

"Actually those who can do. One of our sons has autism. The other two, who are 14 and 17, work when they aren't in school. My husband is a full-time student taking an overload of courses. A lot of the people who come here work, many of us at full-time, professional jobs. Many of the people standing in line here work more than full-time in the service industry."

The next week the pastor's mother smiled at me as I waited for my food. And of course she asked the inevitable, "How's the job search going?"

I replied, "As well as can be expected in this economy."

I made a couple of friends, Laurie (her real name) and Sally (a pseudonym), who were honest with me about their situations. That helped both them and me. To have someone to commiserate with, particularly about the relentlessly exhausting struggle to find ways to pay the bills, made that relentlessness easier to bear.

We struggle. But perhaps we are more honest about it with each other than the general run of citizens are. Even now, it is a struggle. Some months there is a choice between having power and having water. Still. Our extended families don't really want to know. I have siblings with multiple properties whose savings fall easily into six digits. They are good people. They could write a $20,000 check without missing it. They don't visit, but they do call. When they come to town they genteelly ask to meet at a restaurant; they buy. I'm sure they feel good about that. I know they do. They're kind people, they truly enjoy getting together, going out to eat. They would not enjoy walking through my door into the 1200 square foot concrete block house with no heat, window units for air, and 1970's tile floors; with six people living in limited space, along with the two dogs which help with the autism in the house. They don't, really, want to know.

Our mother ages and there are discussions about moving her into a facility, or into one of their comfortable homes out of state. She can no longer clean her own house, and she's too friendly to hire someone to do it. I do it. On top of struggling to get by. Although my siblings do visit, and engage as much as possible, it doesn't occur to them to scrub her toilet. That's a job for me—the poor one. Of course. But we don't talk about that.

And that is what is wrong, here. People don't want to know. That's why I wrote Ana. I'm active in the local arts community; there's a world-class facility close by where I've studied several times. I like the staff out there. They like me. But we argue a bit on facebook when I try to make the local cool people see; this town relies on a workforce which is largely unseen. If you drive the causeways at 1a.m. you will see weary food service workers making their way home, some walking eight to ten miles home. They don't have cars and they don't have insurance. Yet visiting writers are shepherded to the four star restaurants, poured eclectic glasses of vino under twinkling lights while these people ruin their shoes back in the dish-pit. The busboys and dishwashers take the scraps home, wondering if they'll get sick from recooking the leftovers of a $60 steak. It's true. And nobody talks about it.

When my father spent a couple of weeks in a nursing home prior to his death I became acutely aware of how easy it would be for someone who'd carefully set up their life for comfort after retirement to become deeply impoverished. What would a long illness do to finances? What if one lost his insurance, and his job, during that time? My father, like myself, had chosen public service over riskier, higher-paying positions in the private sector. He left my mother, while not rich, safe and comfortable due to his retirement and government insurance. He was a rocket scientist. Time and again he was offered high-paying jobs with private companies, time and again he turned them down. I began to see why as I watched my mother cope with the complexities of the healthcare system. What would happen to somebody with a long-term illness who lost their job before achieving retirement, or vesture in social security? What would happen to their family if the surviving family members hadn't worked long enough to qualify for social security or retirement? Ana was born.

Since I've been working on this book, I've noticed all sorts of places where people can eat, shower, sleep. For example this week my sister was visiting with her family from Sandy Hook, Connecticut. They always stay at a large (twenty building) condominium complex in Bethune Beach, the model for Haven Beach. The complex has several clubhouses and two pools.

Near the pools are locker rooms. In the locker rooms are showers, complete with soap and shampoo dispensers, and shower doors—individual stalls. Although the complex is gated for cars, and you need a pool tag to swim, anyone could walk in from the nearby beach, enter the restroom, and take a shower and change.

At the local hospital, here, each floor has a family waiting room with comfortable chairs and couches, reading material, televisions, and telephones. The nearby restrooms for use of visitors have showers within the individual stalls. The hospital cafeteria furnishes free coffee and tea for visitors to the hospital, 24 hours a day, on a help-yourself basis. Every mile or so along the public beach are free outdoor showers and indoor, individual restrooms with sinks, toilets, and lockable doors. The local supermarkets offer both free coffee as well as free mini-meal samplers throughout the day and evening hours. All of the banks have help-yourself coffee. Many also put tea and cookies within easy reach of anyone walking in the door. One has a popcorn machine. There are ATMs in the lobbies, so one could feasibly check a card balance and help themselves to a beverage and snack.

The most bewildering thing about this book is, *how did she do it?* As you might imagine, dear reader, it's complicated. Here are some key points:

➤ Ana and Frank never owned the beach house. They always rented it from Catherine, Ana's friend in New Jersey. When Ana "moved" to Florida, Catherine was having a terrible time keeping the house clean after renters left. Since Ana had always done her own cleaning when she rented from Catherine, and done an excellent job, Catherine asked if she wanted to keep the house clean between renters—and prepare it for Catherine's own annual deep clean—in exchange for a free month there, every year.

➤ When Ana sold the house in New Jersey, she had only $900 left after paying off Frank's medical bills. She knew she couldn't continue to live in New Jersey. She had no real job skills and no high school diploma, and would not survive a Jersey winter without shelter.

➤ Ana had enough friends who were widowed, and who'd discussed it with her, to know that widowhood was a peculiarly single status which often rendered the widow invisible or at least boxed into preconceived notions. She knew that if she were to chameleon into another life now was the time.

➤ Ana was able to keep herself relatively safe by using the beach house as a base—since she knew when renters were there and when it was empty—and becoming an active volunteer at places where she could sleep. She slept at the hospital, she slept at the church, she slept at the University. If she had nowhere to stay, she slept at the beach during the day in her sun shelter and walked the streets and causeways at night or lingered at the gym and the library; or the all-night study room at the University.

➤ Ana was able to use others' preconceived notions to hide in plain sight. She also used her widowhood to keep a safe distance from her new acquaintances in the town of Robinson. Stashing her winter things with her children, keeping her hair short and her clothing simple, and doing her laundry along with the volunteer smocks at the hospital all helped to keep her both clean and not over-burdened with personal items at any given time.

➤ Ana planned, very carefully, to actually have a "home" or a home base one quarter of the time. For the month of July she had the beach house. She spent ten days a year in a sleeper car on a train going to and from Bellingham, where she spent two weeks. She spent a week every year in Asheville and two weeks at church camp in the Florida Keys. Although she preferred not to, Ana could get away with sleeping at the beach house when it wasn't rented.

➤ When she wasn't traveling or at the beach house, Ana spent Monday nights at the University; Tuesdays sleeping the afternoon away in her cabana at the beach and Tuesday nights at the gym and University library; Wednesday sleeping at the church following cleaning the kitchen; Thursday at the beach in the cabana, followed by staying awake at the University gym and library; Friday working in the ER, followed by sleeping in the locker room; Saturday working in the locker room through the late morning and early afternoon, then working again Saturday night and sleeping in the locker room until time for church; Sunday night sleeping at the church following cleaning up of the kitchen.

➤ Although she didn't like doing it, several times during storms Ana slept on the enclosed back porch of one of the Jackson rental houses down the street from the beach house. She had to be careful not to be seen by neighbors, but both the schedules of the houses she stayed at and those of the neighboring houses were easy to check; they were Jackson houses with their occupancy calendars listed online at the realty's website. Even so, Ana was careful to both arrive and exit under cover of darkness.

➤ During a hurricane Ana's third year in town she used a large chunk of her savings to spend four days at the Bella Vista. The island was evacuated and although shelters were opened on the mainland, Ana had a terrible cold and didn't feel up to keeping up her persona. She took advantage of Bella Vista's "buy three, get one free" deal for prior customers. The stay cost Ana $143.

➢ Ana rarely paid for food. She ate for free at the hospital several times a week; in a pinch, she simply took advantage of the free cup-o-soup and coffee and tea in the cafeteria. She also ate four meals a week free at church; Sunday night, Monday morning leftovers; Wednesday night, Thursday morning leftovers. On Wednesdays she treated herself to a bagel at a local bagel shop for 54 cents, which put 46 cents into her savings account using her debit card—resulting in a cost of eight cents for the bagel. She also shopped carefully for snacks and cans of soup and tuna on Wednesdays: at one supermarket the store brand of soup was 52 cents, but the cans were heavy so she left them stashed in her locker at the hospital. Tuna at another market was 60 cents a can, costing only 10 cents after her bank rounded up. Ana always bought fresh fruit, as close to 51 cents a purchase as possible, on Wednesdays.

Kate Cumiskey is a social justice advocate, writer, and teacher in coastal central Florida. She works to eliminate subtle prejudices in the professional world as well as the general public through her writing and seminars designed for specific groups: for example, teachers working with students with Autism Spectrum Disorders; educators pushing families to reveal private socio-economic status in order for schools to gain funding; and advocates pairing homelessness with drug addiction and mental illness. Cumiskey and her husband Mikel work together to provide homeless individuals with what homeless individuals actually need: homes. She holds degrees from the University of Florida and the University of North Carolina, Wilmington, and is currently a student at Arizona State University where she also teaches. Her work appears regularly in peer-reviewed journals and fine literary magazines. Despite the political turmoil and ravishment of Florida, Cumiskey holds a deep love for its fragile lands and waterways, flora and fauna. She works with local governments to control growth and meet the needs of a beautifully diverse population in schools and in her community. Ana is her fifth traditionally-published book.

www.ingramcontent.com/pod-product-compliance
Lightning Source LLC
Chambersburg PA
CBHW032007010726
47493CB00007B/2313